Assault And Buttercream

LEXY BAKER COZY MYSTERY SERIES BOOK 16

LEIGHANN DOBBS

Chapter One

"CRIME IS REALLY GETTING out of hand here in Brook Ridge Falls." Mona Baker put the small-town paper down on the café table and pointed at the headline.

Lexy Baker turned from where she had been straightening the white ceramic mugs at the coffee station in her bakery to look at her grandmother. Mona, or Nans, as Lexy called her, was seated at one of the café tables next to the large window with her three senior-citizen friends.

Beyond them, Lexy could see Main Street with its old brick stores, colorful awnings, and planters full of lush flowers. Across the street, the waterfall sparkled in the sunlight, and right in front of the bakery, sparrows searched for crumbs around the wrought iron cafe tables she'd put out on the sidewalk.

Nans's three cohorts, Ruth, Ida, and Helen, leaned over the paper.

The four of them came to the Cup and Cake right as Lexy opened up on most mornings to sip coffee, eat pastries, and discuss recent town events of interest. Unfortunately, the events that typically interested them had to do with crime, which often led to investigations, which often led to the four of them getting into trouble.

"A robbery at Farraday Jewelers? That's the second robbery in a month," Ida said.

"Maybe Ruth should ask Vinnie about it," Helen joked. Just a few weeks ago, the four of them had gotten involved in solving a murder related to the robbery of an estate. During the investigation, Ruth had reconnected with an old friend of hers, Vinnie, who was now in prison for that robbery.

"Too bad it's just a robbery." Ida sat back in her chair and bit into a chocolate cupcake with Swiss buttercream frosting. Lexy was trying the recipe out and had asked for Ida's opinion.

Ida chewed thoughtfully, wiped a smudge of frosting from the corner of her mouth, glanced up at Lexy, and gave a thumbs-up for approval before taking another bite.

"Yeah, robberies are kind of boring." Nans sipped her coffee. "But seeing as there's been no murders, maybe we should keep our investigative skills sharpened by trying to figure out who the culprit is."

Lexy grabbed a coffee pot and went over to top off their mugs. She liked to keep tabs on their plans and felt it was her duty to try to steer the ladies out of danger, though they didn't often listen to her. When they got it into their heads to investigate a murder, things could get dangerous. A simple robbery would be a refreshing change of pace.

"That's not a bad idea," Helen said. "I need to launch my own investigation over at the senior center."

Ruth frowned. "Why?"

Helen leaned in and lowered her voice. "Someone has been stealing K-Cups from the pantry."

The other three gasped. "Stealing from our own pantry?"

Helen nodded and sat back in her seat. "Can you believe it? I mean, I have free coffee every Saturday; you'd think that would be enough. As president of the senior center, I feel like it is my duty to find out who it is."

"Indeed. And what kind of punishment will you give them?" Ida seemed excited to hear about what that might entail.

"Well, I don't think I'll punish them. You know the saying 'you catch more flies with honey than vinegar.' I'll see why they are stealing. Perhaps there is a reason. Maybe we can work with them. At the very least, I'm going to let them know that I know so that they don't do any more stealing."

"Maybe it's the same person who stole the diamonds from Farraday's." Ida pressed her lips together and squinted as if thinking. "I do remember hearing a car squealing into the development a few nights ago around eleven. Is that when the heist happened?"

"Yes, that woke me up too." Nans's eyes sparkled with delight. "Do you think the thief could be living in the Brook Ridge Falls Retirement Community?"

The four seniors lived in a fifty-five-plus community

with an active senior center. The community was quite large, with apartment buildings and single-family homes.

"It would make our job a lot easier. I think we should snoop around," Ida said.

Nans bit into the cupcake she'd had in front of her. It was frosted with Italian buttercream.

"Yum! This is good." Nans nodded to Lexy. "Is this what you're using for the dog show."

"One of them. We're planning a few types of frosting, and we've been working on some dog-shaped cupcakes and cookies. Of course, there will be a big cake for the party after the winners are announced." Lexy was excited about getting the contract to cater the desserts for the annual dog show. The show was quite a big deal, with cash prizes for the winning dogs, and the catering contract paid well, not to mention providing exposure for her bakery.

Ruth bit into her sample and nodded enthusiastically. "This one is a winner."

"I agree," Ida said. "Are you entering Sprinkles in the show?"

Lexy laughed. "Sprinkles? Are you kidding me? I can barely get her to sit still."

Sprinkles was Lexy's white Shih Tzu–poodle mix. She was a sweet dog, and Lexy loved her, but she wasn't quite dog-show material.

"It's probably just as well that you aren't entering her," Ida said. "Barbara Morrison's dog, Prudence, is a favorite to win, as is Edwina Southwick's pug, Queenie. They're very competitive about it."

"It's no wonder. There is a ten-thousand-dollar prize for the winner," Nans said.

"Still. They almost came to blows the other day at the hair salon while discussing whose dog was best." Ruth shook her head at the memory of the inappropriate behavior.

Helen pointed her cupcake at Lexy. "You don't want to get in the middle of that, that's for sure."

"You can say that again. I don't think Sprinkles would pass the behavior category, but she is pretty. Which reminds me, she has a grooming appointment in half an hour. I'd better get going if I want to get her there in time."

"We'd better get a move on too. We need to get some intel on this robbery. I say we pay a visit to Farraday Jewelers just as soon as we finish these cupcakes," Ida said as she reached for a strawberry buttercream frosted cupcake.

Chapter Two

LEXY'S favorite place in the world was the kitchen in her small bakery. It was where she could immerse herself in the creation of delicious treats and where the smells of sugary baked goods permeated the air most strongly.

Her assistant, Cassie, was busy mixing frosting in a large stainless steel bowl. She had on a vintage apron with cherries on it, and her pink-tipped, spiked hair bobbed up and down as she vigorously turned the spatula.

On the long steel table in front of her sat various cakes, cupcakes, and cookies in dog-related shapes: bones, dog faces, paw prints. They'd been experimenting with how to make a three-dimensional dog out of cake for the dog show, but judging by the way the one they'd tried earlier in the day had collapsed into crumbs, they needed more practice.

"What are those four up to?" Cassie nodded toward the front of the shop.

"They're disappointed at the lack of murders to investigate. I think they're going to settle for looking into the diamond robbery down at Farraday's."

Cassie straightened and frowned. "I heard about that. Kind of weird, don't you think? I would have thought they'd have heightened security given how much those loose diamonds were worth."

"No kidding. I'm sure they have insurance."

Lexy grabbed a small tasting spoon out of the drawer. Was it coincidence that someone had broken into the jeweler's when it had just gotten a big shipment of diamonds? She imagined the loose stones would be easier to get rid of than if they were in settings, and with insurance, the jeweler wouldn't lose out on much. Could it have been an inside job for insurance money?

She shook her head. She had no intention of getting involved in the ladies' investigation. She had the dog show catering to focus on, and since it wasn't a murder, she figured they couldn't get into too much trouble on their own.

"Is this the Swiss buttercream recipe?" She dipped the spoon into the frosting then popped it into her mouth, closing her eyes as she twirled it around on her tongue. The buttery-sweet taste was perfection.

"Yep." Cassie stood back, watching Lexy's reaction.

"This came out great. Can you do a batch of chocolate?"

"You bet."

"Thanks. You're a lifesaver." Lexy removed her gingham apron and hung it on one of the pegs on the wall next to the door. "I need to take Sprinkles to Doggie Diva for a ten-thirty drop-off to be groomed. Can you watch the shop for a while?"

"Sure. I'm done with this batch of frosting, so I'll go out front in case customers come in. It's still early, so we won't have many customers."

"Perfect. Thanks." Lexy headed out the back, calling over her shoulder, "Don't let Nans and the ladies eat all our profits!"

Sprinkles was more than happy to go for a ride in the car, so it didn't take Lexy long to get her out of the house and drive to Doggy Diva.

The little dog seemed eager for the adventure, but as soon as Lexy let her out of the passenger seat of her small yellow Volkswagen Beetle and started toward the front door of the salon, the dog started to act funny.

"Come on, Sprinkles, you usually love this place." Lexy tugged the leash while backing toward the store. She loved the look of its fluffy poodle sign in turquoise and its white-and-pink-striped awning.

Sprinkles tugged back, holding her nose in the air and sniffing.

"Okay. I promise I won't let them put the bright-red nail polish on." Lexy had thought it looked cute, and it matched the bow they'd put on her the last time she'd been groomed. Sprinkles had had a different opinion though. She'd acted almost embarrassed, hiding her paws every chance she got.

Sprinkles edged closer but looked uncertain about entering the shop.

"Come on, now. I have to go back to work. I promise I'll be back this afternoon to get you." Lexy coaxed the dog forward. She opened the door with one hand while pulling the dog inside.

The lobby was weirdly silent. Usually, there was someone behind the desk or just coming out of the back, and often, another client was either picking up a freshly groomed dog or dropping one off. Maybe Kelly, the groomer, was wrestling with an uncooperative canine out back.

Sprinkles whined, her gaze intent on the counter, and Lexy got the ominous feeling that something wasn't right.

She glanced toward the door behind the counter that led to the back but didn't see any sign of movement. "Hello? I'm here for Sprinkles's appointment!"

No one answered, so she edged closer to the counter.

Sprinkles whined and pulled in the opposite direction.

"Hello, anyone back there?" she yelled more loudly.

No answer.

Lexy sighed. She didn't want to be a pushy customer, but she wanted to get back to the Cup and Cake before the lunch rush. Maybe she should just pop into the back...

But wait! What was that smudge on the corner of the counter? She bent closer. It looked like blood!

She rounded the corner. Someone lay behind the counter!

She recognized the form as Freddy Lang, who worked part-time at Doggy Diva.

She dropped Sprinkles's leash and fell to her knees beside him, desperately feeling for a pulse.

Lexy's heart sank, because there was no pulse. Freddy Lang's blank eyes stared at the wall. His fingers were curled around the handle of a blue leash, but the collar at the other end was empty.

Had he been bringing a dog into the back? And where was that dog now?

"What's going on?" Kelly Farmer, one of the groomers at Doggy Diva, stood on the other side of the counter, looking confused as to why Lexy was crouching behind the desk. Lexy realized that from her vantage point, Kelly couldn't see that Freddy was lying on the ground in front of her.

Before Lexy could answer, Kelly's expression turned apologetic. "I just ran out to grab something to eat. Freddy was supposed to be here. I hope you haven't been waiting long."

She started toward the counter, but Lexy held up her hand. "No need to apologize. You might not want to come back here—there's been an accident."

"An accident?"

"Unfortunately." Lexy whipped out her phone. "I'm going to have to call the police."

Kelly's eyes widened. "The police? What kind of accident?" She peered around the side of the counter, where Freddy's feet, clad in his trademark high-top sneakers, were clearly visible. She drew in a sharp breath. "Is that Freddy? Is he… is he…?"

Lexy nodded as she talked to the police dispatcher.

Kelly seemed completely distraught. "Oh, no, this isn't good. Poor Freddy. What kind of accident could be that severe?"

Lexy didn't answer. She'd wait for the police to investigate. She'd told Kelly there had been an accident because she wasn't sure what she should say, but judging by the way the back of Freddy's skull was smashed in, his death had been no accident.

Chapter Three

Lexy did her best not to interfere with the crime scene while she waited for the police. She was married to homicide detective Jack Perillo, so she was quite familiar with what she should and shouldn't do at a crime scene. Her knowledge of crime scenes wasn't only because of Jack though; she had happened across an unusual number of crime scenes with her grandmother.

Truth be told, she would have liked to poke around a bit, but Kelly was very shaken, and Lexy spent most of the time sitting beside her in the lobby, trying to comfort her.

Two Brook Ridge Falls police cars pulled up, and Lexy got ready to answer questions.

Jack was first through the door. He had a concerned look on his face until their eyes met and he saw that she was okay. Dispatch must have told him that Lexy had called in the crime, and she imagined the good-natured ribbing he would get about her drumming up business for him later on. But her heart did a little flip to know that he still cared that much.

Sprinkles's heart must have done a little flip too, because she ran toward Jack, her tail wagging as she greeted him as if he'd just come home from work with a steak in his hand.

"Hey, Sprinkles." Jack bent down to scratch behind her ears, his lips curving in a slight smile despite the serious reason he was there in the first place.

"Sprinkles, come!" Lexy grabbed the leash and pulled her back then addressed Jack. "Freddy's behind the counter."

Jack's face was grim as he proceeded to the counter along with the four other officers that had arrived. The presence of the police seemed to calm Kelly down.

Jack gave instructions to the others as they processed the scene. He looked over the countertop and then opened the cash register. "Looks like they weren't after money." He glanced over at the empty end of the leash. "A dognapping?"

"Or maybe the dog got loose? I haven't seen a dog running around," Lexy said. "I tried not to touch too much though. He could be scared and hiding in back."

"Are any dogs missing from the back?" Jack asked Kelly. His voice was gentle as he came to stand in front of them.

"I don't know. I had stepped out to get lunch, and Freddy was the only one here." Kelly's eyes darted to the door that led to the back kennels, from which sounds of barking and whining were filtering out. The only way to get there was to step over the body. "I really should check on the dogs." Kelly looked at the front door. "I can go outside and get in from the back entrance. If I'm allowed to leave."

"Yes, of course you are. I'm interested to see if any dogs are missing." Jack gestured toward a female officer, who Lexy recognized from her various trips to the police station. "Officer Kennedy can take you."

Kelly and the officer disappeared out the front door, and Jack turned his attention to Lexy. "Did you see anything unusual? Anyone driving away when you got here? Any idea of who might have done this?"

Lexy was surprised that Jack seemed to have confidence in her powers of observation. Usually, he would simply warn her away from getting involved. Maybe she'd finally proven herself to him after all the clues she and her grandmother had given him on other cases. Unfortunately, she had no clues to give him on this one.

She shook her head. "Nothing. The only things I noticed were the same things you did: the smudge on the counter and the empty leash." Lexy thought for a minute then added, "But there is that dog show coming up, and it does have a big cash prize. Nans and the ladies said that two of the contestants have been arguing over whose dog is best. Do you think this could be related?"

"Maybe." Jack's narrow-eyed gaze slid to the body, which crime-scene techs were loading onto a stretcher.

"You don't think it was an accident, do you?" Lexy indicated the corner of the counter.

Jack shook his head. "He could have fallen against it

and gotten hurt, but it would take extensive force to cause the injury on the back of his head. He was pushed with force and on purpose."

"Oh dear. But why?"

"Maybe Freddy here had some enemies?"

"Maybe. I don't know much about him except that he works here a few days a week. I guess he's a big dog lover, but I have no idea if he might have enemies. I guess that's for the police to investigate," Lexy said.

Jack's gaze snapped back to her. "That's right. And not you and your grandmother, right?"

"Of course not," Lexy assured him, but her mind was already nagging her about different clues to chase down and suspects to interrogate. "Besides, Nans and the other ladies have already set their sights on investigating the diamond robbery down the street. I'm sure that will keep them very busy."

Over at Farraday Jewelers, Nans, Ruth, Ida, and Helen were peering into the display cases, pretending to peruse the jewelry. Whenever the sales clerk wasn't looking, they darted glances toward the corner of the store that was roped off with yellow crime-scene tape.

"Aquamarine is my birthstone," Ida said. "So I think that's what I'm going to look at." She scuttled off over toward the display case that happened to be near the crime-scene corner.

"I'll help you look, Ida!" Nans hurried after her.

"I'm a pearl girl myself." Ruth headed for the pearl display, motioning for Louise Farraday to follow her. Her job was to distract Louise so the others could get a look at the area where the stolen diamonds had been on display.

"Are you looking for something in particular, Ruth?" Louise asked. Her eyes brimmed with suspicion as she tracked Ida, Helen, and Nans on the other side of the room.

"Just a simple choker, I think. I'm just comparing prices for now," Ruth said just in case Louise might expect her to actually buy something.

She let Louise show her three different necklaces, which she draped on a black velvet tray. The pearls all had a lovely creamy luster and looked fabulous set against the black. Ruth was just wondering if maybe she should spring for one—the one with the ten-millimeter pearls would look great with the new black dress she'd bought for her special date—when the others joined her at the counter, signaling that they were done with their observation of the area.

"Sorry about the diamond heist," Nans said. Nothing like making it obvious.

"Yes, it was quite a shock." Louise glanced over at the corner.

"Looks like you had a lot of diamonds. I bet they're quite valuable," Ida said in her usual blunt manner.

"You must have had them locked up pretty tight though?" Ruth asked.

Louise nodded. "Of course we did. That section of the store is under a special laser-light security system."

Everyone looked over to the corner.

"Apparently not special enough," Ida said.

Louise frowned. "Well, we thought it was. We worked with Lowe's Security specifically to have it installed. It has laser beams that crisscross, and if a beam is broken, the alarm goes off."

"But no alarm went off?" Nans said.

Louise pressed her lips together and shook her head.

"How do you figure the thief got into the store though?" Helen asked. "Maybe this is like the Broadmoore heist a few weeks ago, where people used special skills to bypass the security."

Louise shook her head. "I don't think so. That was a private residence. This is a store, and we have the best security systems in place."

All three ladies just stared at her.

"Well, obviously, someone used *some* skill. They'd have to get into the store and then bypass the laser security for that case." Louise pointed to the corner again.

"So you have a laser-light system on the case but not the doors?" Nans asked.

Louise bristled. "We have an alarm and a lock and key, of course. It's all we've ever needed."

"And a camera." Ruth pointed to the security camera tucked into the corner near the ceiling. "It didn't catch the thief?"

Louise's cheeks colored. "Unfortunately, there was a glitch. The stupid thing has been glitching out for weeks now. My brother, Douglas, was supposed to see to it that it was fixed and then beef up the door security, but he didn't do a very good job of that."

"So the camera glitched during the time of the robbery. Did it come back on later?" Nans asked.

"It was off and on all night, but the diamonds were there at ten thirty and missing after midnight."

"How convenient for the thief that it glitched right when the robbery took place," Ida said.

"The police seemed to think it was quite a coincidence."

Nans gave the others a knowing look. "Yes, quite a coincidence indeed."

Chapter Four

LEXY HAD WAITED PATIENTLY in the front room of Doggy Diva for Jack to finish his investigation of the scene. She knew he might have some additional questions for her, and she wanted to be as helpful as possible. Sprinkles wasn't quite as patient, however, and Lexy was debating whether she should grab a package of dog treats from the display rack and leave some cash on the counter when the owner, Carl Newtson, came rushing in.

"What's happened here?" He tugged at his collar, obviously upset.

Lexy stood. "I'm afraid there's been a death, Carl."

Carl's face turned white. "What do you mean? A customer?"

Lexy thought it was strange his mind would go there. He looked as if he was more worried about a lawsuit than his own workers considering that he hadn't even asked about Freddy or Kelly.

"It was Freddy Lang," Jack said, coming around the counter to stand in front of Carl. "He was murdered."

Carl gasped. "Murdered? Are you sure?"

Jack nodded, his expression grim. "Where have you been? Do you often leave your workers alone in the store?"

"I'm just getting in to work. I had errands to run this morning. I have people to run the shop, and I'm not here all the time." Carl sounded a little miffed.

"So you haven't been here at all today?" Jack asked.

Carl's gaze darted around the room. "No, why?"

"Just asking. It seems that there may have been some foul play."

Just then, Kelly came back through the front door. "All of the dogs are accounted for."

Carl looked confused, so Lexy explained. "Freddy had a leash in his hand with no dog at the other end, so we thought maybe it was a dognapping."

Carl swiped at a bead of sweat that had formed on his forehead. "Dognapping? Why?"

Lexy shrugged. "I don't know. I thought maybe it had something to do with the dog show. There's a big cash prize, and I've heard there have been some arguments among the contestants already."

"Well, I wouldn't know anything about that. Thankfully, all of our clients are accounted for back there. But poor Freddy. Oh dear! I'll have to see what I can do for his family. Will the shop need to be closed down?" Carl craned his neck at the crime scene behind the counter, and Lexy could picture the wheels turning in his head as he counted the money he would lose.

"Not for long. We've processed most of the scene already. Should be wrapping up in a bit." Jack was staring at Carl as if mentally adding him to the suspect list. "In the meantime, I'm going to need you to look around and see if anything is missing. There is money in the cash register, but I don't know if it's the right amount. Is there anything else of value here in the store?"

Carl glanced at the display shelves. "Dog supplies, leashes. Some of the dog food is expensive, but there's nothing worth killing someone for."

"Do you have a safe in the office?" Jack glanced at a door to the right. "We haven't looked in there yet."

Carl jerked his head in that direction. "It's locked. The door isn't broken down, so I imagine they didn't get in. There's no safe in there."

Carl pulled his keys out of his pocket and rushed to the door. He unlocked it and stuck his head in then turned back to Jack. "It's just as I left it. Nothing's disturbed. Even my laptop is still on the desk."

Jack nodded. "Okay. I'll let you know when we finish up and you can open."

Carl went into his office, and Jack came over to Lexy.

"You don't have to wait around. If I have other questions for you, I know where to find you." Jack winked at Lexy then bent down to pet Sprinkles.

"Okay, see you tonight." Lexy gave Jack a peck on the cheek and tugged on Sprinkles's leash. Answering more questions wasn't the only reason she had been staying. She wanted to eavesdrop on the investigation because she had one burning question...

If no dog had been taken, then why was Freddy clutching the leash?

Carl stood behind his desk, wiping sweat from his brow as he brought his surveillance app up on the computer. He could never figure out how to work the darn thing properly, and he was very nervous, which wasn't helping.

He clicked on the mouse and banged on the keyboard but couldn't get the videos from earlier in the morning to play. It didn't really matter though; he knew what was on the one from the camera pointed at the lobby. Unlike what he'd told Detective Perillo, this was not the first time he'd been there that day.

Perillo had a reputation for being thorough, and Carl was sure his next step would be to ask about the surveillance footage. Luckily, Carl was known for being on the cheap side, and it was common knowledge that many businesses put up fake cameras that didn't actually record anything.

And even though he didn't know how to play back the video, he did know how to get rid of it.

He squinted at the screen that showed what was happening right now. His stomach lurched as he watched the police dust for fingerprints and take pictures of the floor behind the counter.

Wait, did that bakery woman just kiss Perillo?

He didn't have time to spy on them. He navigated to the directory with the stored videos.

Delete!

Delete!

Delete!

By some miracle, he figured out how to reconfigure the directories so it looked as if only the camera at the back door worked. Now he could give that file to the police, and it wouldn't show a thing.

He didn't need the police scrutinizing his business any further than they already were, even if it meant a killer might go free.

Chapter Five

LEXY RAN INTO NANS, Ruth, Ida, and Helen on her way out of Doggy Diva. They were coming from Farraday Jewelers and were practically running down the sidewalk.

"I heard there were police cars at Doggy Diva. What happened?" Nans asked.

The promise Lexy had made to Jack about not investigating with her grandmother flitted through her mind, but she couldn't very well *not* tell them. They'd find out soon enough on their own. And besides, telling them wasn't the same as investigating. "Freddy Lang has been murdered."

Nans gasped. "How exciting. I mean, how terrible. Are there any clues?"

"I hope you looked over the crime scene carefully, Lexy. You know how important it is to get eyes on the scene before the police take everything away."

"I did." Lexy liked investigating these things as much as her grandmother, though she wouldn't admit that to Jack. "There was something very unusual about the scene."

"What?" All four ladies leaned in closer, their eyes as big as moon pies.

"Freddy was clutching a leash in his hand so tightly that they could barely get it out of his grip, but the other end of the leash didn't have a dog attached."

"Really? How odd is that?" Ruth asked.

"Whose dog leash was it?" Helen asked.

"It's unknown at this time," Lexy said. "All the dogs were accounted for."

"Well, did you look at the calendar to see who was scheduled?" Ida asked.

"I couldn't exactly do that. I don't even know where they keep it," Lexy said.

Actually, she hadn't even thought to do that but didn't want to admit it to the ladies. Now she was kicking herself. If she had, she could have nosed around on the desk while she was there, but since she hadn't, maybe she would be able to get the information out of Jack later that night. The shop probably kept the calendar online though, and it wouldn't have been smart to touch the computer.

"Maybe you'll be able to get that out of Jack," Ruth said, eerily echoing her thoughts.

"You guys aren't thinking about investigating, are you? I mean, you must have your hands full with the diamond theft." Lexy figured she would make an effort to dissuade them, since she'd promised Jack.

Ida waved her hands. "Theft? This is much more important and exciting. It's our duty to make sure killers don't just run around town."

"Besides, we can investigate both, can't we?" Ruth asked.

"Of course we can," Nans said. "We're retired and have all day long with nothing to do."

"We have a third investigation too," Helen said. "We need to find out who has been stealing the K-Cups from the senior center."

The other three gave Helen "the look."

"What? It's a legitimate theft."

"We'll see what we can do about that," Nans said. "In the meantime, let's get back to my place and fill out the whiteboard. Will you meet us there, Lexy?"

Lexy had some extra time, since she wouldn't have to pick up Sprinkles after her grooming. Even though Jack had said Carl could reopen, Sprinkles would miss her appointment. Lexy couldn't stop the ladies from investigating as Jack had asked, but at least she could keep an eye on them. "I guess so. I'll just drop Sprinkles at home and be right there."

"Don't be afraid to swing by the bakery and bring some of those double-chocolate-dipped biscotti!" Ida yelled as they hurried off, their large patent-leather purses swinging from their elbows and sensible shoes scuffing the pavement.

Chapter Six

BY THE TIME Lexy got to Nans's apartment in the Brook Ridge Falls Retirement Community, her grandmother had already rolled the giant whiteboard into the dining room and was jotting down clues.

Ruth, Ida, and Helen were sitting at the mahogany dining table. A carafe of coffee sat in the middle of the table, and each of the ladies had a dainty porcelain teacup and saucer as well as a dessert dish in front of her.

A variety of K-Cups were lined up on the table in front of Helen. She was systematically peeling off the tops, pouring out the coffee grounds, and replacing them with something else.

"Helen, what are you doing?" Lexy asked as she slid the bakery box onto the table. She'd stopped by the Cup and Cake on her way to Nans's place. She'd learned that showing up without pastries usually didn't go over very well, especially with Ida.

Ida dove for the box, pulled it toward her, and lifted the lid.

Helen peered at her over the rim of her red-plastic reading glasses. "Someone's been stealing the K-Cups from the senior center, and I'm creating a little trap to catch them."

"She's replacing the coffee with dandelion tea," Ruth said.

Helen nodded. "I figure I'll put these fakes in the storeroom, and whoever is stealing them will complain about the coffee. Then I'll know who the thief is. Have you ever had dandelion tea? It's gross."

"I suppose that could work." Lexy remembered having dandelion tea once, and the taste was quite different from coffee. But would the culprit actually complain about coffee pods they'd stolen?

"Never mind about that. Let's see what Lexy brought." Ida reached into the box and pulled out one of the smaller boxes Lexy had packed inside. This one held a dozen dog-shaped cookies. They were from the batch that Lexy and Cassie were making for the dog show, but they hadn't quite made the cut because they had minor imperfections. Lexy wasn't going to tell that to the ladies, though.

"Aren't those cute!" Ruth took one and put it on her plate.

"And check out these." Ida pulled out a small box of cupcakes with dog ears on top and a tail sticking out of the side.

"They're for the dog show. Do you like them?" Lexy always liked to get the ladies' opinions of her new pastries.

"Of course!" Helen bit into a cookie.

Ruth patted crumbs from her lips. "They're cute."

"Taste good too," Ida mumbled.

Nans looked over at the table from where she was standing at the whiteboard with her dry-erase marker poised above the surface. "They're adorable. Except for that one that is missing the ears and the other one that has no eyes. Did you find out anything more about the crimes?"

Lexy looked at the whiteboard. Nans had two columns, one for the robbery and one for the murder. She didn't have very many clues or suspects written down so far.

"I haven't heard anything more," Lexy said.

"Did you bring any biscotti?" Ida asked.

Lexy grimaced. "Sorry, we were sold out."

"Ladies, let's try to keep on topic." Nans tapped the whiteboard with her pen. "Let's go over the robbery. So far, we know it happened between ten thirty p.m. and midnight."

"How do you know that?" Lexy asked.

"Louise said it had to be then because the surveillance system had had a glitch during that time," Ruth said.

"And she also said someone would've had to get into the store in the first place. And how could they know the camera wouldn't be working?" Ida added.

"Maybe they didn't even know there was a camera," Lexy suggested.

Ruth made a face. "Now that I think of it, I heard a car careening through the development just before midnight that night. I know the time because I checked my clock."

"You were up then too?" Ida asked. "I was getting a

little snack, and I saw that car. It was Barbara Morrison. I recognized her Jeep."

"Barbara Morrison?" Lexy asked. "That name seems familiar."

Ida held up a dog bone–shaped cookie. "Probably heard of her in relation to the dog show. Prudence, her Pekingese, is a favorite to win."

Helen looked up from her task of securing the K-Cup cover back on. She was using some kind of glue. Lexy hoped it was edible. "That furry thing? It looks like a mop."

"But she always puts her hair in that cute bow on top of her head," Ruth said.

"Ha! I've seen her grandson, Larry, walking that dog, and he looks a bit embarrassed when it has the bow on." Ida selected another cookie.

"Yes, but he's a nice boy to walk the dog for her, don't you think?" Helen asked.

"I agree. I like a man who isn't embarrassed to walk a froufrou dog," Ruth said.

Helen turned to her. "You also like one who isn't embarrassed to wear a leotard like Mario Blondini used to wear when he was in the Circo Acrobato."

Ruth blushed and looked down at her plate. Ruth had developed a soft spot for one of the suspects in their last case. It had turned out that Mario was cleared, but since he'd been Helen's competitor for president of the senior center, she couldn't help teasing Ruth.

"I highly doubt Barb would be involved with the jewelry theft," Nans said. "She doesn't need the money."

Helen nodded. "She's not in the dog show for the money, unlike Edwina. She doesn't really *need* the money either, but she's greedy. Now take Millie Dixon—there's someone that really needs the money."

"Still, I think we should make a note to visit Barbara. We need to do a thorough investigation of every clue." Nans's pen squeaked across the whiteboard. "You never know what you might find out. She may have seen something while she was out."

"Mona! You don't really think that someone who stole those diamonds would be here in the retirement complex, do you? I mean, it's one thing to steal K-Cups." Helen held up the K-Cup she was currently working on. "It's another to steal diamonds."

Nans pressed her lips together. "I suppose you're right."

"What about the murder?" Ida waved her cookie at the other side of the board. "We don't have very much to go on there. We may need to call on Lexy to use her special influence with Jack."

Everyone looked at Lexy.

"I do happen to know one thing." Lexy was pleased she had some information the ladies hadn't dug up yet. "Carl, the owner of Doggy Diva, acted kind of strange when he came in and discovered what had happened this morning."

"Well, it is upsetting to find a dead body in your place of business," Helen said. "Could make one act strange."

"I know, but there was something off about his behavior. I think there's more to it."

Nans's eyes narrowed. "Do you think the murder has something to do with the dog show?"

"It does have a big prize, but not big enough to kill for. Then again, one never knows," Lexy said.

"It could be a lot of money to some. To some, even stealing K-Cups is worth it." Again, Helen held up the K-Cup she was working on.

Nans shoved the cap onto her pen. "I think we have enough for now. I say we get to the fieldwork. We should visit Barbara Morrison right away. We can make the excuse that we want to show off Lexy's dog-shaped cookies. Since she's competing in the dog show herself, maybe she'll know something."

Chapter Seven

BARBARA LIVED a few streets over from Nans in one of the single-family homes in the senior development. They boxed up some of the dog-shaped cookies and a few cupcakes and headed over on foot.

Her house was a modest ranch with brick siding. The grass was neatly mowed, the trim freshly painted a bright white, the window boxes brimming with colorful flowers.

As they approached, the door swung open, and Barbara came running out. She skidded to a stop when she saw them in the walkway.

"Prudence is missing!" She wrung her hands, looking quite distressed.

"Missing?" Ida asked. "What do you mean? Maybe she just trotted off to the neighbors."

"Trotted off? I don't let her just trot off!" Barbara frowned at Ida. "She's kept indoors. She has her own bedroom and is taken out on the leash for potty. I'm sure someone has taken her on purpose. She's been stolen!"

"Stolen?" Lexy flashed to the crime scene. "Did she have a blue leash?"

"Blue? No." Barbara looked close to tears. "She was wearing her pink hair ribbon, and I always coordinate, so her leash was pink, and it's still here. She'd just had a bath and brushing... I hope she isn't being mistreated. She is very sensitive."

"Now, slow down." Nans placed a comforting hand on Barbara's arm. "What time did you last see her?"

"Just this morning. I fed her her special breakfast—she gets a proprietary blend, including dog supplements with green-lipped mussels and antler velvet for her joints." Barbara's eyes darted around the yard as if searching for the dog.

Ida had wandered over to the shrubs and was looking behind them. "Nothing back here."

"Do you think she could have gotten out somehow?" Nans asked. Barbara was no spring chicken. Maybe she'd had a memory lapse and left the door open.

Barb twisted around to look at the door. "No. I'm very careful."

"Okay, let's go back over the events of the morning," Nans suggested.

Barb closed her eyes. "I got up around five and took Prudence out to do her business then made my usual poached egg. Then I prepared Pru's breakfast and served it in her crystal dish. Then I brushed her."

"And you were home all day?" Nans looked skeptical. If Prudence hadn't gotten out by accident and Barb was home all day, how could someone have taken her?

"Oh! No. That's right. I had to pop out to the mall to get more ribbons for Pru's hair. I was running low." Barb's eyes popped open wide. "That's it! Someone took her while I was at the mall!"

Helen glanced at the front door. "Was there a break-in?"

"No. I don't think so. The front doors were closed, and Pru didn't come trotting out as usual. I looked everywhere —in the tub, out the back. I checked under all the beds; she likes to hide under there sometimes when she's naughty."

"Then how did someone get in?" Nans asked.

Barbara looked sheepish. "Well, to tell you the truth, I never lock the front door. We have so little crime here."

Everyone nodded. Even though Brook Ridge Falls seemed to have more than the average number of murders, there were hardly ever any break-ins.

"But who would steal her?" Ruth asked.

Barb's eyes narrowed. "Who? Ha! I'll tell you who. Edwina Southwick, that's who. She's desperate to win the dog show and knows Queenie can never beat Prudence because Queenie is too hyper to win the obedience contest. If it wasn't for that, Queenie would actually be tough competition for Pru. What better way to make sure she knocks out the competition than to eliminate it by stealing Prudence!"

"I guess that's a possibility..." Nans glanced around at the rest of them to see if they agreed. Ruth and Helen looked skeptical. Ida's attention was on the bakery box.

"Maybe we should think about this more over some cookies." Ida held the box up.

"Cookies?" Barbara asked.

"We brought some samples that Lexy made at her bakery. They're for the dog show." Ida flipped the top up and took a dog bone–shaped cookie out. "Aren't they cute?"

Barbara waved off the cookie, and Ida shrugged and bit into it herself. "I don't have time for cookies. I need to get to the police and report Prudence's dognapping right away!"

"Police?" Nans looked interested. "Lexy's husband is the homicide detective in town. We have an in with the police. Let us escort you, and we'll make sure they give this matter the attention it deserves."

"Oh, thank you very much." Barbara seemed truly grateful.

Lexy hesitated. Jack liked to help the people in town, but he was a homicide detective. A missing dog wasn't exactly his purview. But Nans had that determined look on her face. She never missed an opportunity to visit the police station, where she might be able to glean information on a case she was working on. Lexy figured her grandmother was more interested in snooping around to see if she could find anything out about the robbery or the murder.

As they headed toward Barbara's garage, where her black Jeep was parked, Ida turned to her. "Are you sure Prudence was there this morning? I mean, someone entering your home in the daytime is unusual, but under the cover of darkness, it makes more sense. And I saw your car racing through the development at midnight the other night."

"Midnight? Don't be silly. I'm in bed way before then, and anyway, Pru was here this morning." Barbara seemed genuinely confused. "I'm not the only one with a black Jeep. If you're worried about people lurking around the neighborhood at night, maybe you should worry about Millie Dixon. I saw her skulking around down the street, near the entry to the senior center, at two a.m. last week, and I'm sure she was lurking around my backyard the other night!"

"Two in the morning! What were you doing out then?" Helen asked.

"Prudence had an upset stomach. She'd eaten a magnet." Barbara sighed. "She's a good girl but will eat almost anything. I'm trying to break her of it. Anyway, it was a lucky thing she passed it easily."

Ida made a face. "Yeah, lucky thing."

Barbara frowned. "Come to think of it, Millie might have been surveilling my place so she could steal Prudence. She has a dog in the show too, you know." Barbara leaned toward them and lowered her voice. "And I hear she has money problems. Her dog, Winston, could have a shot at the big prize if Prudence was out of the running."

"Oh, dear. Well, it sounds like we have several suspects already. We'd better get to the police station and let Jack sort this out. I do hope that Prudence is okay. Are you okay to drive? Maybe we should take Ruth's car."

Lexy cringed at the thought of taking Ruth's car. It wasn't that Ruth's antique Oldsmobile wasn't big enough for the six of them; it was. It was more that Ruth's driving skills weren't exactly up to snuff. So when Barbara said she would drive and Ida made a fuss about it being too crowded, Lexy volunteered to ride with Barbara.

As she sat in the passenger seat, she didn't have time to worry about how many mailboxes Ruth hit or how many curbs she drove over. She was busy thinking about the missing dog and the murder that morning at Doggy Diva and wondering if the two incidents were related.

Chapter Eight

"CAN you describe the kidnap victim? Height? Hair color? Eyes?" Jack was being a good sport about the dognapping. He'd ushered them into a conference room with barely a raised brow at Lexy and had listened to Barbara's story intently. Lexy knew he was doing it mostly for her, and it warmed her heart. She made a mental note to bring a special dessert home from the bakery for him.

"She's about ten inches tall, with long blond hair and soulful brown eyes." Barbara sniffed into a tissue.

"And she was last seen at your house?" Jack asked.

Barbara nodded. "Yes. She wouldn't leave on her own. She's a good girl."

"Do you have a picture?"

Barbara took a silver-framed photo out of her purse and handed it to Jack. "This is when she won the blue ribbon at the Westchester Dog Show last year."

Jack frowned. "Dog show? We're having one here in town this week."

Barbara leaned forward. "I know. Prudence was favored to win. That's why someone took her!"

Jack glanced at Lexy. She was curious to know what he thought. Mention of the dog show appeared to cause him to take this more seriously, but did he see a connection to what had happened at Doggy Diva? She would have to ask him when they both got home. Usually, he was reluctant to let her in on police business, but she had her ways of getting information out of him.

"I'll show this picture around and have everyone on the lookout." Jack patted Barbara on the arm. "Don't worry. We'll find her."

He stood and gestured toward the door, and they all filed out of the room.

"It's always so nice to visit the police station, and you're always so helpful, Jack," Nans said. Even though she was talking to Jack, her eyes were darting into all the offices they walked past, trying to spy a clue about the cases they were working on, no doubt.

"Thank you, Mona." Jack stopped in the doorway to his office.

"Your office is always kept so neat!" Nans pushed her way in, her eyes going immediately to the corkboard, which had several photographs on it.

Lexy couldn't help but look too. The board held a picture of a pile of diamonds, a black-and-white still photo of what looked like a car bumper with a small dent in it, interior photos of the jewelry store, and a closeup of the lock with scratches on it.

"Oh my, did someone pick the lock?" Nans pointed to

the photos. "We talked to Louise Farraday just this morning, and she said the door only had a lock and an alarm, but additional security was inside the store."

Barbara had stopped her sniffling and was staring at the photos. "What's all that about?"

"Break-in at Farraday Jewelers," Nans said.

"Funny that there's a break-in and a murder in the same week!" Ruth added.

Barbara gasped, her eyes still glued to the pictures. "Someone was murdered at Farraday's?"

"No, that was at Doggy Diva. Poor Freddy Lang," Helen supplied.

"Freddy?" Barbara looked quite upset. "Oh dear, he was such a nice boy."

"Indeed." Nans said. She was no longer looking at the pictures but was craning her neck toward the hallway outside Jack's office. "Well, we should be going."

Nans rushed out into the hall just as the door to the interrogation room shut. She looked back at Lexy and raised her brows then hustled toward the exit. Clearly, she'd seen something of importance.

"What was that about?" Jack asked as the other ladies shuffled off behind Nans.

"One never knows with my grandmother." Lexy gave him a quick peck on the cheek. "See you at home for supper?"

"Of course!"

Lexy hurried out to the parking lot. Ruth, Ida, and Helen were in the Oldsmobile, and Nans was riding shotgun in Barbara's Jeep, so she slipped into the backseat.

"Are you okay to drive, Barb?" Nans asked.

"Yes."

"You seemed a bit upset about the robbery and murder."

"Well, of course. It's just that nothing like that ever happens in town, and here I am leaving my door unlocked. It's disturbing."

"You can say that again." Lexy snapped her seat belt into place. "What was going on in there, Nans, when you bolted out into the—"

Smash!

Lexy jerked forward in her seat.

Nans twisted around in her seat to look out the back window. "Oh dear! You hit the sign."

"Oh no!" Lexy unclipped her seat belt. "Let me go see if there's any damage."

"No. Don't worry, dear. It happens all the time. These darn eyeglasses." Barb took her glasses off and looked at them then placed them back on her face and angled her head to look in the side-view mirror. "The sign seems to be okay."

Lexy looked out the back window. The sign was still standing, barely a scrape on the metal pole. "It's fine."

"Okay, then let's just be on our way. There's plenty of dings in the old bumper. What's another one?" Barbara put the car into gear and drove off. "Now, what were you asking about, Lexy?"

"Just that Nans seemed very interested in the hallway when we were in Jack's office."

Nans turned in her seat, a mischievous twinkle in her

green eyes. "When we were talking to Jack, I saw his part-
ner, John, walking down the hall. He was going to the
interrogation room, and guess who he had with him."

"Who?" Barb and Lexy both said.

"Douglas Farraday. It looked like they were questioning
him about the stolen diamonds."

Chapter Nine

MILLIE DIXON SKULKED along the hedges separating Barbara Morrison's property from that of the Millers next door. She didn't want anyone to see her, least of all Barbara. It wouldn't do to have someone discover the secret path in the woods that Millie was sure only she knew about.

The Millers were in Europe, and she'd seen Barbara go out with a gaggle of other seniors. But still, the grandson, Larry, often came to visit, and she certainly didn't need him asking any questions.

"Come along, Winston. We mustn't let anyone see us," Millie whispered as she tugged the little dog along behind her. Winston was a Papillon and a gentle and obedient little pet.

Ducking into the woods, she breathed a sigh of relief when she slipped between the branches of the evergreens and the large shrubs. Now no one could see her.

She had a path that she took frequently to pick her

herbs for the herbal remedies she made. She knew exactly where the dandelion, foxglove, and lemon balm were. She knew which herbs to take and which to stay away from.

Luckily, Winston also seemed to have an ingrained instinct for the herbs. He knew not to touch the ones that would be poisonous and could have adverse effects on him, like the very rare and endangered indigo nightroot that was...

Wait a minute. Where was the indigo nightroot? The patch used to be right here, growing in the swampy area after the second downed oak, where the large hen-of-the-woods mushrooms grew. But the area where the indigo nightroot had been for years was empty.

How was that possible?

She picked her way around tall ferns, telling Winston to stay near the oak tree. She didn't want him anywhere near the area. Even though there were no plants, there could still be traces of the essential oils. The indigo night-shade could be a helpful sedative in small doses, but large doses could be toxic for dogs.

Now she could see that the area had been rooted up as if an animal had dug in there. A bear, perhaps? She'd never seen this happen before, but there was always a first time. Maybe a badger or bobcat. But further inspection proved her wrong. This was no bear, badger, or bobcat. There was a distinct imprint of a boot in the mud. A *human* had been in here, digging up these plants, but who?

Suddenly Millie felt scared. Someone else knew about her secret place. She glanced around the woods, which had always felt friendly, but now she envisioned shadows lurking behind every tree.

Whoever had been out here could get into a lot of trouble for digging those herbs up. Now more than ever, she needed to make sure no one knew she came to this section of the woods. She might get blamed for digging them up. She didn't have any money to pay a fine; she could barely pay her rent as it was.

She hurried away from the area, taking the path that led to the far side of the forest, and came out near the police station. "What do you make of that, Winston?"

Winston gave a soft yip in reply.

"I know? Who would do that and *why*?"

But as she asked herself the question out loud, her mind was already forming an answer, and suddenly, she had an idea of what it was all about. The problem was how she could prove it without exposing her own suspicious activities.

Chapter Ten

BARBARA BACKED the Jeep into her garage and closed the door. She'd dropped Lexy and Mona off at Mona's apartment and hadn't been able to get rid of them fast enough. It had been nice that they'd accompanied her to the police station, but now she had a lot to think about.

She walked around to the back of the jeep and looked at the bumper. The dent was a good one and had changed the look of the bumper, since it was placed over one of the dents that used to be there and next to the other dent from when she'd backed into Shirley Robinson's car at the grocery store. That had been almost a year ago, and Shirley still hadn't let her forget about it. She'd gone on and on about it then in the parking lot, even though her car had barely received a scratch, and managed to bring it up almost every time Barbara saw her.

As she approached the door to the house, her heart felt heavy because she knew that Prudence wouldn't be there to greet her. Had she done the right thing? It didn't matter now. What was done was done. After what she'd seen and heard at the police station, she figured it was better safe than sorry.

She took a deep breath and opened the door. There was no shrill bark and no clicking of tiny claws on the linoleum. The bag with the ribbons she'd purchased that morning sat on the counter. Barbara took out the pretty pink polka-dot one, holding it in her hand as tears rolled down her cheeks. She'd envisioned using this bow in Prudence's hair at the dog show this week, and now...

She shook her head and brushed away the tears. She must focus on positive thoughts. Who would harm a fluffy little Pekingese? Maybe that depended on why she was taken. Surely Millie or Edwina wouldn't harm Prudence. They just wanted her out of the way for the show.

And unlike what Mona and her gang had implied, Prudence *had* been home this morning. Barbara's memory wasn't that bad. Though they had a point; it would have been smarter for someone to take her in the middle of the night, especially since Barbara took those great sleeping pills that knocked her out cold. Someone could come right into the house and cook an entire meal, and she probably wouldn't wake up! But no, Pru had been there this morning, so someone had been bold enough to take her in broad daylight!

Her gaze came to rest on a picture of Prudence and her grandson, Larry. He was such a good boy—no, "boy" wasn't right... he was a man now, almost thirty, but Barb still thought of him as a boy. He was sweet and helpful, always doing things around the house for her. And he loved Prudence.

He'd be very upset to discover she had been kidnapped. She almost hated to tell him. He was probably still reeling about Freddy Lang's death; Larry and Freddy had been good friends. And now she hated to heap this on him too. Her instinct, as always, was to protect him. But now that she thought about it, maybe Larry wasn't as good as she'd always envisioned. She did like to put him up on a pedestal, as her friends always told her.

Oh well, one had to break the bad news sometime, and she could sure use Larry's comfort right now. She took a deep breath and picked up the phone.

Chapter Eleven

"I BROUGHT YOUR FAVORITE DESSERT." Lexy held the white bakery box stamped with the pink Cup and Cake logo out to Jack. He was standing at the counter, taking the stuffing out of tiny little Cornish game hens. The hens were a specialty of his, and Lexy's mouth watered at the sight of the crispy skin and the smell of roasted chicken.

Sprinkles sat next to him, looking up expectantly. The food prep explained why Sprinkles hadn't run to the door to greet Lexy as usual.

Jack lifted the lid and peeked inside. He smiled. "Boston cream pie? Thanks." Then his expression turned suspicious. "What's going on? Usually, when you bring my favorite dessert, there's an ulterior motive."

Lexy laughed as if he were joking, though she knew he wasn't because it was true. "I just wanted to thank you for being so nice to Barbara Morrison about her missing dog. It was really sweet how you took the time to talk to her about the dognapping." That was true as well.

By now, Sprinkles had realized no food-prep morsels were going to fall to the floor, so she bounded over to Lexy, who scooped her up in her arms. Lexy's heart pinged with sympathy for Barbara as Sprinkles covered her chin in dog kisses. She didn't know what she would do if someone took Sprinkles. "Do you have any leads on the dog?"

Jack shook his head. "No. I gave copies of the photo to everyone so we can be on the lookout during patrols. No one has called in about a stray dog wandering around."

"I hope they find her. Do you really think someone stole her? Maybe someone will contact Barbara for ransom money."

Jack looked dubious as he put the Boston cream pie on the counter and turned back to plating the chickens. "Maybe. Barbara mentioned that she thought someone might be trying to get Prudence out of the way, but it seems a little excessive to steal the dog for a dog show, don't you think? I mean, the prize isn't *that* much."

"You never know with these older ladies. They can be very competitive," Lexy said. "But it does seem off. Even for a ransom, how much could they get? Seems too risky for the reward. I just hope the little dog is safe." Lexy buried her face in Sprinkles's fur. Yech, wet-dog smell. "I think I need to make a new appointment at Doggy Diva. Sprinkles missed her grooming, and she really needs one. Do you think it's safe to go there?"

Lexy wasn't really worried about whether it was safe; this was the perfect segue to get Jack talking about the murder investigation.

"I'm sure whoever killed Freddy did it for personal

reasons. It's not like there's a maniac killing people in the lobby of the dog-grooming spa." Jack put the plates on the table and gestured for Lexy to sit. "Though that Carl Newtson seems a little sketchy, don't you think?"

"He was acting weird this morning." Lexy poured two glasses of wine and put them on the table.

"Do you know him well?" Jack asked.

This was a switch. Jack was asking *her* for information when it was usually the other way around. If she played her cards right, maybe she could get some information in return.

"Not very well," she said as she carved some meat from the tiny chicken. It was juicy and the skin perfectly crispy. "He usually stays in the office. I have heard that he pushes the envelope a little, though I have no specifics. Why do you ask? Do you think he was involved in the murder?"

"I wouldn't say we think he's involved, but he claims some of his surveillance cameras are broken and don't record. Specifically the ones in the lobby, where Freddy Lang was murdered." Jack pushed some meat and stuffing onto his fork. "Seems odd because Freddy worked for Lowe's Security as his second job, so you'd think Carl would have him fix the cameras."

Lexy's left brow ticked up. "Oh, really? Wasn't there something funny about the surveillance camera at Farraday Jewelers?"

Jack nodded. "Very observant of you. Yes, there was. It was glitchy."

"Do you think the two crimes could be related?"

"I would never rule anything out, but so far, we haven't

found any relation. Sometimes coincidences are just coincidences."

Lexy chewed thoughtfully for a few minutes, then she took a swig of wine, "You know, what bothers me the most is that leash. Why was Freddy holding the leash?"

Jack's eyes were guarded, but he nodded. "It is a mystery. We have a leash with no dog attached and also a missing dog with no missing leash."

"Barbara said Prudence's leash wasn't blue, but maybe she was confused."

"We think the leash came from the store. There were two missing from the display, according to Carl."

"Two?"

Jack nodded. "We didn't find another one lying around, but we can do forensics on the blue one and might be able to determine whether it's one of the missing ones or not."

"Really?" That was impressive but not surprising. Hadn't Lexy seen something similar on a *CSI* episode? She wondered about the missing leashes though. Maybe Carl was saying things were missing from the store to cash in on some insurance settlement.

"I called Barbara to bring in some hair from Prudence to see if the leash was used for her. You wouldn't believe the information we can get. Mold spores, pollen, all kinds of things."

"We don't know if Freddie had a dog on the leash or was going to get one from the back. But it was too early in the day for anyone to be picking up a dog because pick-ups happen in the afternoon, so why would he be getting one?" Lexy mused.

Jack watched Lexy as she took another bite of the stuffing. "Do you like that stuffing? I put raisins, pineapple, and walnuts in it."

"Delicious," Lexy mumbled around the mouthful. She figured she might as well keep asking questions, since Jack appeared to be in a talkative mood. "Any leads on the jewelry heist?"

Jack looked up and smiled. "I think I've given you enough information. You know I don't like to talk about the cases. Word always seems to get back to your grandmother, and the last thing I need is for her and her cabal to put on their trench coats and launch investigations into these crimes."

Darn. She'd known Jack would clam up sooner or later, but it had been worth a try.

"They don't actually wear trench coats," Lexy joked. "But you may be too late. Nans saw Douglas Farraday at the police station when we were there earlier today. Is he a suspect?"

"Just because he was at the station doesn't mean he is a suspect," Jack said. "We bring people in there to tell them things, too, you know."

"Oh, so you had something to tell him?" Lexy persisted.

Jack smiled over the rim of his wine glass. "Nice try, but I'm not going to tell you why Douglas was there."

Lexy knew better than to push, and she understood that he couldn't share specifics about cases with her. She focused on finishing the meal and turning the conversation to safer topics about their day. By the time they broke into the Boston cream pie, the discussion had turned to what they were doing the next day.

"Tomorrow is Saturday, and I have it off," Jack said. He alternated weekends off with the other detectives. "I'm playing golf in the morning, but maybe we could take Sprinkles on a hike in the afternoon."

"I have to cater the senior center coffee hour in the morning. Apparently, Helen's campaign promise of free coffee on Saturdays also included free pastries from my bakery."

Jack laughed. "Leave it to Helen to wrangle that out of you. I guess it's good advertising."

"I suppose." Lexy really didn't mind. It didn't cost much for the things she brought, and the senior center residents were some of her best customers. "Then later on, I have to stop by the armory and check out the dog-show setup so I can see how to arrange the area they have for my pastries."

"Sounds like you have a full day."

"Oh, and Helen has a thief who's stealing the coffee pods. I'm sure she's going to be up to something tomorrow to try to narrow down her suspects. Maybe you'd like to come along and help?" Lexy teased.

Jack rolled his eyes. "No thanks. I think I'll catch up on my reading. I'm sure Nans, Ruth, Ida, and Helen can figure out who the coffee culprit is without my assistance."

Chapter Twelve

HELEN HAD SET up the Brook Ridge Falls Retirement Community Center nicely for the free coffee she'd promised during the campaign.

Chairs were arranged around round tables with simple bud vases in the middle. The front of the room was decorated with green and blue streamers. A row of tables was set up along one wall. The tables were draped in plain white linen and held two coffee carafes, two K-Cup machines, a stack of Styrofoam cups, and crystal bowls with individual sugar packets and small containers of cream. Next to that was an area for Lexy's pastries.

Lexy had brought her usual assortment of muffins, Danishes, and cupcakes. She'd even included a tray of the dog-shaped cookies that she was making for the dog show.

"These cookies are so adorable!" Myra Bertollini reached toward the tray, a diamond bracelet on her wrist sparkling in the light.

"Myra! Is that a new bracelet?" Sheila Baldwin pointed at the sparkly gem.

Myra beamed as she held her wrist up for inspection. "Yes, it is. Henry got it for me."

Sheila gasped. "But it must have been so expensive. Is it zirconia?"

"Genuine diamonds," Myra purred. She leaned toward Sheila and lowered her voice. "Jeffrey's Jewelers is having a big sale on diamonds. If you want your Gus to buy you something, I suggest you take him down there today. Things are going fast."

Ruth and Ida rolled their eyes as the two ladies gushed over the bracelet.

"I'm more interested in the cookies." Ida picked up a cookie decorated to resemble a Boston terrier and bit into it. "Excellent."

"Thank you so much for bringing the pastries, Lexy," Helen said. "It really makes a big difference, and everyone loves them. I hope they bring in some business for the Cup and Cake."

"It's no trouble," Lexy said. She actually wasn't sure if it brought her any extra business, but she didn't mind; she liked seeing the seniors enjoying her pastries.

Ida stood on her tiptoes and craned her neck toward the coffee area. "Have you seen anyone stealing coffee?" she whispered.

Helen shook her head. "Not so far. But surely you don't think the thief would be so bold as to steal right here with everyone watching."

Ruth shrugged. "I don't know. Sometimes it's better to

sneak around in plain sight."

"Yeah, I guess that's what Millie Dixon figures." Ida jabbed Nans in the ribs and nodded toward the end of the table, where Millie was shoving a cheese Danish into her purse.

Nans laughed. "I hope you're not going to imply that she's doing something shady. You put pastries in your purse all the time."

Ida made a face. "Yeah, but that's the third one she's taken. At least I wrap mine. She's going to get gooey cheese and icing all over everything inside her bag!"

"Now now, don't be too hard on Millie. She's fallen on hard times." Mario Blondini had come to stand in their little group. Not surprisingly, he was right beside Ruth. Nans, Ida, and Helen raised their brows at how close the two were standing. Ruth blushed.

"Hard times? I wonder what kind of coffee she likes." Helen glanced toward the coffee station again.

"I highly doubt that she's your coffee thief. The thief is breaking in to the senior center at night and stealing the K-Cup pods," Lexy said. "There's a pretty big difference between putting a Danish in your purse and breaking and entering."

"She might have some good breaking-and-entering skills if she's like the rest of the Circo Acrobato." Ida turned to Mario. "Just what did she do in the Circo?"

Mario cleared his throat. "I don't think Millie is a thief. She's one of the family."

"Family schmamily. What are her skills?" Ida asked.

"Well, she was one of our best acrobats. She could

contort herself into the smallest of spaces, escape from chains and locked boxes, and was a star on the trapeze." Mario glanced over at her and frowned. "But that was in her younger days. She's much older now. And many of us older acrobats have lost our skills." Mario looked regretfully at his fingers, which were gnarled with arthritis.

Ruth patted his arm.

"She was an escape artist? Then she can probably pick locks," Helen said.

Mario laughed. "Well, all of us can do that. Who can't pick a lock?"

"Excuse me, Helen." Ramona Farmer shoved her way into their little group and gave Mario the once-over.

Ruth frowned.

"Hi, Ramona," Helen said. "Do you need something?"

"We're out of creamer." Ramona pointed toward the coffee table, exposing a pair of jangly diamond-studded bracelets on her wrist.

"Are those new bracelets?" Nans asked.

Ramona twirled the bracelets around on her wrist. "Yes. Real gold and diamonds."

"You don't say," Ida said. "Did you get them at Jeffrey's Jewelers?"

"Yes. How did you know?"

Ida shrugged. "I heard he was having a sale."

"I'll get some creamer right away," Helen said.

As Helen and Ramona headed off, Mario excused himself to talk to Millie. Nans, Ruth, Ida, and Lexy tightened up their circle.

"I think this business with Jeffrey's Jewelers is something to check out," Nans said. "It can't be a coincidence that he's running a sale on diamond jewelry when Farraday's was just burgled!"

"I agree." Lexy glanced at Ruth uncertainly. "And I get a funny feeling about Millie."

Ruth seemed slightly offended on Mario's behalf. "Millie's harmless... I think."

"Maybe. But the locks at Farraday Jewelers were picked. If she can pick locks and contort herself and do gymnastics to get around the laser alarm system, then we might want to add her to our suspect list," Nans pointed out.

Ruth sighed. "I guess we should keep her in mind. But she's old. She might not be that flexible anymore. I'll see what I can find out."

"Good thinking. And I say we go to Jeffrey's later today." Nans turned to Lexy. "Are you in?"

"I can't. I have to go to the armory for a trial run of the dog-show setup."

"Oh, that's good. You might be able to find something out about the murder. I'm sure it has something to do with dogs."

"And maybe even catch up on the incident with Barbara's dog, Prudence," Ruth said. "There must be more to that. In fact, I still swear it was Barbara's car I saw speeding down the street."

"Sounds good. How about we meet back at the bakery around five tonight and compare notes?"

"Good idea." Ida picked up another cookie. "Don't forget to save us any leftover pastries!"

Chapter Thirteen

THE ARMORY where the dog show was being held was about the size of a hockey rink, with an open area that was perfect for the show. Most of it had been set up when Lexy arrived, but in a few spots, people were huddled together discussing placement of various items.

The open area in the middle was divided into two sections. One was empty, and Lexy assumed that would be the judging ring in which they would parade the dogs and present the awards. The other side had ramps and cones and hurdles used for dog agility. Grooming stations were set up around the ring, and many dog owners were setting up the tables and arranging their dogs atop them.

As Lexy understood it, only one category of dogs would be in the ring at a time, and the other dogs would be at their stations. Judges would go around to each dog individually, inspecting their appearance, temperament, and stance.

Lexy placed the long dachshund-shaped cake on the

table and stood back to see how it looked. It would have benefitted from a cake stand, but it was too long to fit on one. Maybe she should have made a Chihuahua instead. Still, the cake looked so realistic with its brown icing and candy eyes and nose that the thought of cutting into it made her squeamish.

"That's the last of the items in the van." Cassie placed a covered container on the table and pulled on a pair of pink latex gloves to help place the items.

Even though this was just setup rehearsal for the dog show and there wouldn't be a crowd or audience, Lexy and Cassie had brought an abundance of samples so they could see how the table would look against the backdrop of the large armory. It wasn't that the bakery was being judged or anything—they'd already been hired—but Lexy still wanted to make a good impression.

She moved the triple-tier stand loaded with cupcakes and lined a white tray with doilies. Then she and Cassie arranged the cookies on the tray.

"That should do it," Lexy said.

Anastasia Winters approached. She was dressed in a tailored magenta suit and had her silver hair swept up on top of her head. "Lexy! Cassie! These baked goods are adorable."

Lexy relaxed. Anastasia was the head judge and the main organizer for the dog show. Her approval meant a lot because she put a lot of events together, and if she liked the job Lexy and Cassie did, then more catering events might come out of it.

"Thank you. We have three types of buttercream

frosting on the cupcakes: American, French, and Swiss." Lexy pointed to each type of cupcake in turn.

"Sounds delicious." Anastasia reached out for the cupcake with the Swiss buttercream. It was a vanilla cupcake with vanilla frosting fluffed up like dog hair. Two pink-sugar ears stuck out of the top, and the front had a candy nose and eyes.

"Delicious!" Anastasia wiped some frosting off the corners of her lips. "You brought so much. You really only needed to bring a little bit so I could stage the room and see how everything fit in. But since you have so many items, why don't you invite some of the dog owners and other judges to grab some pastries while you are walking around to check things out. Could be good for business."

Lexy didn't mind if she did. She loved dogs and was eager to see some of them up close. Plus she wanted to see if she could shake out some information about Prudence's disappearance or the murder at Doggy Diva.

There were all kinds of dogs: poodles, German shepherds, golden retrievers. Lexy spent time with all of them, talking to their owners, wishing them good luck, and pointing them toward the food table.

Most of the owners were dismayed to hear about Prudence's kidnapping. The area where Barbara would have set up to groom and display Pru sat empty, a reminder of the sad occurrence.

"Does Jack have any leads on Prudence?" Cassie asked as they paused at the empty table.

"No. It's worrisome. I hate to think of that poor little dog all alone and scared."

"Hopefully, whoever took her isn't harming her." Cassie was truly concerned.

"I'm not sure she was kidnapped. I mean, who would do that? And Barbara might not be that reliable. She swears that Prudence was locked inside, but I have some concerns about Barbara. She smashed into one of the signs when we left the police station, so maybe there's something going on with her."

"She was probably just nervous about her dog." Cassie's gaze shifted to the back of the room. "Most of the people we've talked to seemed genuinely concerned for the dog's welfare, but I bet a few people are glad. With Prudence out of the way, it opens up an opportunity for winning the small-dog category."

Lexy followed Cassie's gaze. Edwina Southwick and Carl Newtson were huddled together in the back corner, whispering animatedly about something.

"I heard Edwina and Barbara had an argument about whose dog would win," Lexy said.

"Me too. Queenie is cute, but she's kind of hyper. She never shows well." Cassie pointed to a small pug dancing around on the table nearest Edwina.

"I've seen Queenie at Doggy Diva. She's not very well behaved. I wonder what Edwina and Carl are talking about. It looks serious."

"Looks like they're arguing."

Just then, Edwina glanced over. Her eyes locked on Lexy's, and she scowled before jerking her attention back to Carl.

"I don't know why Edwina would think that Queenie

would be next in line after Prudence. My money would be on Winston." Cassie nodded toward a table on which a beautiful white-and-brown papillon sat obediently. Winston was also looking at Edwina and Carl. His long, silky hair cascaded out from his large ears, which were standing at attention.

"Winston is a very nice dog. Much less hyper. And so obedient, just sitting there all alone." Lexy scanned the room for Winston's owner, Millie Dixon, but didn't see her. That was odd.

Lexy didn't know about Winston, but she'd never trust Sprinkles to sit obediently unattended for too long, especially when there were cupcakes and cookies on a table nearby. Which made her wonder, where was Millie, and why had she left her dog alone?

CARL LOOKED into the angry face of Edwina. He wished he'd never gotten mixed up with her, but it was too late now.

"That nosy Lexy Baker has been asking questions," Edwina whispered.

Carl glanced over at the bakery owner, who was now making her way around the room. He'd noticed her watching him, and it made him nervous. What had she been doing at Doggy Diva the morning the police came, anyway? She'd said she had an appointment for her dog, but still. "I saw her kiss that detective. Perillo."

Edwina gave him a funny look. "They're married."

Carl had a hard time keeping track of who was married to whom. He was much better at figuring out who was cheating on whom and other items of information that he could leverage to his financial advantage. Too bad he wouldn't be able to resort to blackmail with the baker and the detective; he might need something to use as a bargaining chip with the police if they discovered he'd erased those surveillance files on purpose.

Carl prided himself on doing dirty deeds that wouldn't get him into too much trouble. He loved finding unsuspecting victims whose emotions clouded their better judgement. That was why he'd opened Doggy Diva in the first place. People would do just about anything for their pets... even if it meant pushing the limits of the law.

"Don't worry. She doesn't know anything," he assured Edwina.

"As long as the police don't look too closely. I don't want any suspicion to fall on me... or my little Queenie."

Carl glanced at the mangy mutt. He supposed it was a handsome dog with its wrinkly face, curly tail, and large, trusting eyes, but the constant prancing and dancing were distracting. As he watched, the dog seem to get less antsy and finally stopped squirming and sat still.

"That's a good girl, Queenie." Edwina stepped over to the table and patted the dog. Queenie leaned in to enjoy the behind-the-ears scratch, a goofy dog smile on her face.

Edwina glanced sharply at Carl. "We shouldn't be seen together too much. Maybe you should go. I'm going to take Queenie out for a little wee-wee."

Carl couldn't wait to get out of there. He'd only come to the dog show to set up his display materials to advertise the Doggy Diva business. Edwina was the one who had pulled him off to the side. She could be sort of clingy, and he hadn't been smart enough to avoid her. But it was good that she had in a way, as he'd gotten to check on Queenie and make sure things were working as he'd thought they would.

Without another word, he turned and went in the opposite direction of Edwina, using the back exit so as to avoid the nosey cupcake woman.

Millie held her breath and listened for a few more seconds to make sure Edwina and Carl were actually gone. Once she was satisfied, she unlatched the door to the giant dog crate that she'd been hiding in. It was under the table and hidden by the tablecloth, which hung down to the floor, so luckily, no one could see her. She unfolded her legs and spine joint by joint and crawled out. Staying on all fours, she peered over the top of the table. No one was watching.

She stood and brushed off her outfit. Even though she was older now, she was still very limber and could contort herself into small places, unlike poor Mario, who was riddled with arthritis. It was a testament to the herbs she took every morning and the fact that she kept up with the stretches and exercises that she'd done daily when she was in the Circo Acrobato. Being limber and spry proved very useful when she wanted to spy on people like Edwina.

She'd suspected that Edwina and Carl were up to something, and she was right. Not only had their suspicious conversation confirmed it, but her vantage point under the table had given her a view of their footwear. And Carl's boots looked suspiciously like they could have left the footprint she'd seen in the woods.

Now that her suspicions had been verified, she had to figure out how to prove it without shining the spotlight on her own underhanded activities.

Over at her station, Winston was waiting patiently like the good boy he was, sitting on the table, his fur perfectly groomed, his eyes bright. She hurried over to reward him. He deserved to win the dog show, and if she could just prove her suspicions about Edwina, he'd have a good chance. Especially with Prudence missing.

Winning would be a great accomplishment, but the money was what she was really after. If she didn't get an influx soon, she was afraid that things would not be good for her or her darling Winston.

Chapter Fifteen

JEFFREY'S JEWELERS was down an alley in the less affluent part of town. The proprietor, Jeffrey Jones, was a wizened old man who had owned the shop for fifty years after inheriting it from his father, who had inherited it from *his* father. Luckily, all three men were named Jeffrey, and the sign had never had to be changed.

Despite the small size of the shop and the fact that everything looked like it had been in its place since 1970, Nans noticed the store did have an updated security system. She glanced back at the door to see a state-of-the-art security lock and thought it odd that Jeffrey's would be more up to date than Farraday Jewelers. Perhaps that was why the thief had stolen from them instead.

Jeffrey glanced up from his position hunched over a desk. A giant jeweler's loupe was affixed to the left lens of his horn-rimmed eyeglasses, giving him somewhat of a comical steampunk look.

He started to stand, which looked like it was going to

take a long time and be rather painful for him, so Nans put up her hand, palm out. "No need to get up on our account. We're just looking around."

Jeffrey nodded then squinted at her. "Mona Baker?"

"Yes, Jeffrey, it's me and Ida, Ruth, and Helen." Nans pointed to her companions.

"Oh, well then, welcome. I rarely see you ladies in here."

"We don't go for jewelry much," Ida said. "But we've heard around town that you're having a fantastic sale."

Jeffrey smiled and slowly pushed to a standing position despite Nans's protest. His joints creaked and cracked, but it didn't take nearly as long as Nans had thought it would.

"Yes, I've had some great estate items come in at a very reasonable price, and I'm passing the savings along to my customers." He hobbled toward an antique oak display case.

"How nice," Nans said as they all shuffled over to join him. Inside the case lay two necklaces and three bracelets adorned with various gemstones including diamonds. A lone diamond ring sat on a black-velvet ring display that could have held many more.

"Looks like the case has been cleaned out," Helen said.

"I was able to offer good prices, and word gets around quickly." Jeffrey looked pleased.

Ruth's forehead creased. "That's great, but you said this was from an estate?"

Jeffrey nodded and pushed his glasses onto the top of his balding head. Thank goodness, because the loupe attached to them was a bit off-putting, and Nans's attention had kept waffling between his other eye and the loupe. "I get a lot of estate business. It's not unusual when someone passes that the heirs would rather have money than some old jewelry."

"I was wondering about the heirs though. Didn't they want top dollar?"

Jeffrey shook his head. "Poor dear only had one grandson, and he was quite distraught. He wanted the money quickly, even if it meant taking less. Apparently, there were medical bills that needed to be paid."

"Oh, dear, I wonder who it was," Helen said. "I'd like to pay my respects."

"Um... I have the information right here." Jeffrey shuffled over to a pile of papers and started thumbing through them. "Here it is. Eleanor Robinson."

Helen pressed her lips together. "I don't think I know any Eleanor Robinson." She turned to Nans. "Do you?"

Nans shook her head and looked at Ida and Ruth, who both shrugged.

"I believe the grandson said they were from New Ipswich." Jeffrey put the papers down and came back to the display case.

"Oh, well, that is a few towns over, and if she was elderly and ill, we might not know her," Ruth said.

"One can't know everyone, though at our age, it seems like we do sometimes." Jeffrey pulled a ring of dozens of keys out of his pocket and started sorting through them, eyeing the back of the case as if to figure out which key opened it. "Can I show you ladies something?"

It looked as if Jeffrey could take a while, and they really

didn't want to buy anything, so Nans said, "Not right now, dear. We're just taking a look at what's available. We don't make decisions quickly. We'll have to think on it."

Jeffrey looked disappointed. "Okay, but I can't guarantee these will still be here later on. As you can see, things are going quickly."

"We'll take our chances. Thank you." Nans left with the others following.

"What do you make of that?" Ruth asked once they were out on the street.

"I'm not sure. It looked like he had a lot of security, which makes me wonder why Farraday doesn't," Ida said.

"The diamond sale on the heels of the diamond heist is an awfully strange coincidence." Helen glanced back at the store. "You don't think Jeffrey could be lying about where he got the jewelry from, do you?"

Nans pressed her lips together. "We've known him a good long time. He's always been honest. But I guess it won't hurt to check out his story."

"Sounds like a plan," Ida said. "Now, all this investigating has me famished. I say we head to the Cup and Cake to meet Lexy."

Chapter Sixteen

"I KNEW IT! There is no Eleanor Robinson that recently passed away!" Helen held up her iPad, which showed a running list of obituaries.

Nans sipped her coffee. "Not everyone puts their obituary online, but still."

They were sitting in the Cup and Cake with fresh coffees and pastries on the table in front of them. Lexy was cleaning the coffee station beside them as they filled her in on what had happened during their visit to Jeffrey's.

"Yeah, something is fishy," Ida said as she cut a cream cheese brownie in half. She wrapped one half in a napkin and stuck it in her purse.

"Indeed." Helen turned to Lexy. "How did it go at the dog show?"

"My pastries were a hit." Lexy gave the counter one final wipe before sitting at the table. She leaned forward and lowered her voice. "Funny thing though, I saw Carl and Edwina there, whispering in the corner, but that's not the strangest thing that happened."

"What is?" Nans asked.

"You know Millie Dixon's dog, Winston?"

"Yeaaah." They drew out the word and all leaned in closer, their undivided attention on Lexy. Even Ida paused from taking a bite of her brownie.

"He was posed on his grooming table, but Millie was nowhere to be found."

The ladies settled back in their chairs, frowns crossing their faces as they considered this.

"Mario said Millie had fallen on hard times," Ruth said. "But surely she wouldn't abandon her dog in the middle of the dog show."

"One might wonder how she can afford to show her dog in the first place. Dogs are expensive, aren't they?" Helen asked.

"Sprinkles sure is. And if you're showing them, there's the grooming and the brushes and the collars and leashes." Lexy pressed her lips together. "Speaking of leashes, I haven't heard anything more about the one Freddy was holding or the one missing from Doggy Diva. Maybe I can get some more information on that out of Jack tonight."

"That would be good, dear," Nans said.

Lexy's gaze fell on the iPad, on which Helen was searching more obituaries. "You really don't think that nice man that runs Jeffrey's Jewelers was lying about the grandson, do you?"

Helen held the iPad up again. "The Internet doesn't lie."

"True, but maybe there was no announcement. Some families just keep things private these days, and if the only relative was a grandson, maybe he was overwhelmed and didn't print any notifications," Lexy suggested.

"We might not have this right. What if it wasn't Jeffrey that lied? What if it was the grandson?" Helen said.

Ida's brows rose. "Oh, I see where you're going with that. Whoever stole the diamonds might've been fencing them through Jeffrey's, taking the loose diamonds and putting them into settings so as to avoid suspicion."

Nans thought back to when she'd seen Douglas Farraday at the police station. "And who do we know that is the right age to be the grandson of an elderly woman and who also had access to the diamonds and knew how to make jewelry?"

"Douglas Farraday." Ida popped a big chunk of brownie into her mouth. "I always thought it was an inside job."

Ruth narrowed her eyes. "You may be on to something. That glitch with the security cameras was a little too convenient. If Douglas was the thief, he probably arranged for a convenient security glitch."

"That's it!" Helen jumped from her seat.

Everyone turned to look at her.

"What?" Nans asked.

"The security cameras. That's how we'll catch the K-Cup thief. We'll put security cameras up outside the storage room area of the senior center and see who breaks in."

Chapter Seventeen

LATER THAT NIGHT, Lexy and Jack were snuggled together on the sofa, eating the hamburger, onion, and green pepper pizza she'd picked up on the way home.

Sprinkles had claimed her spot right between them and was busy switching her attention from Lexy to Jack, depending on which one of them had a slice in their hand.

Jack fed her a teeny piece of crust. "Did you bring her to the groomer today?"

"No. I couldn't get an appointment until tomorrow." Lexy leaned over and pulled another slice from the pizza. She folded it and put one hand under it to prevent any drips from getting on her as she brought it up to her mouth.

"Oh, good. She is looking a little raggedy."

Sprinkles gave Jack a look as if she'd understood what he'd said and her feelings were hurt.

Jack bent down and kissed the top of her head. "Don't worry. You're still my favorite girl."

Lexy looked at him sideways. "Hey, now."

"Okay, Sprinkles is my second favorite." Jack slid his arm around her shoulders, pulled her closer, and kissed her cheek. "Mona is my first favorite."

"I knew it!" Lexy laughed and slapped at him playfully. Jack used to own the house behind her grandmother, and Nans had known Jack long before Lexy had met him. Nans had tried to fix Lexy up with him several times, but Lexy had always refused. Funny how things turned out.

"Speaking of your grandmother, I see she isn't wasting any time investigating the diamond theft." Jack took his arm back and grabbed another piece of pizza.

"Did you expect anything less? Did she call you?"

"Yes. She mentioned that Jeffrey's Jewelers had a jewelry sale, and a lot of the ladies at the free coffee event this morning had new jewelry." Jack shrugged and took a bite of his pizza.

"She mentioned that to me, but it didn't seem like anything concrete. Do you think she's grasping at straws?"

"Yeah, a little bit. In real police work, we need evidence, not just hunches and coincidences."

"But don't the hunches and coincidences lead to evidence?"

"I suppose." Jack took another bite and chewed thoughtfully.

"Speaking of evidence, have you made any headway with the leash or on Prudence's disappearance?"

"Nothing conclusive. But I asked Barbara to bring in one of Prudence's brushes. We can get her hairs from the brush so we can compare them to clothing on a suspect."

"Do you have suspects?" Lexy was hopeful.

"No. The dognapping isn't really one of our priorities, but I figured she could bring it in just in case." Jack patted his lips with a napkin then balled it up and tossed it into the empty pizza box. "How did everything go at the armory today?"

"It was great. Everyone liked my pastries, but I did see something odd there. Edwina Southwick and Carl Newtson were whispering in the corner, and Winston, Millie Dixon's dog, was there all by himself. I never saw Millie."

"I don't know about Millie Dixon, but Carl is on my radar. And it's funny that you mention him in conjunction with Edwina, because we reviewed the surveillance tapes from the street that Doggy Diva is on. There isn't a camera that points directly at the pet salon, but one points across the street, and Edwina's car was parked there early the morning of the murder. Did you see her when you brought Sprinkles in?"

"No. No one was there when I brought her. I don't know if I noticed Edwina's car though." Lexy picked a green pepper off the slice of pizza she was holding and nibbled on it as she thought. "I don't think Edwina mentioned anything about being at Doggy Diva that day, but I guess I really haven't spoken to her directly."

"Maybe she was just dropping Queenie off for grooming."

"Maybe." Lexy made a mental note to ask Kelly when she took Sprinkles the next day. "Speaking of surveillance, Helen is putting some surveillance cameras in at the senior center to see if she can catch the K-Cup thief in the act."

Jack chuckled. "Maybe that will keep them busy and out of my cases for a while."

"Let's hope so." Lexy doubted that would be the case.

Chapter Eighteen

BARBARA ARRIVED at the police station early the next morning. She parallel parked out front, careful not to back into anything this time.

She reached over and touched the bag on the seat beside her. Inside was Pru's brush, her long, silky hairs still wrapped around the bristles. She choked back a tear as she considered that those were possibly the last parts of Pru she'd ever see.

Anger bubbled up. Who had taken her precious Pru? It was probably that nasty Millie Dixon, who was always touting her Circo Acrobato career as if being in the circus was something to crow about! But then there was Edwina Southwick. She wanted to win badly, and, of course, there was little chance of that with Queenie's behavior issues. She was a lovely dog, very handsome and lovable, but really, Edwina should train her better.

Oh well, no sense in dwelling on it, and she must not lose hope. She had to believe that Prudence would turn up, and if it had been Millie or Edwina, surely they wouldn't stoop to harming the little dog.

At least she still had Larry. Of course, he'd been devastated about Freddy's death and Prudence's disappearance, but he'd still managed to find it in his heart to console Barbara.

Larry was such a nice grandson, she'd do anything for him. Bake him cookies. Lend him money. Let him use her car... though she suspected maybe he used it when she didn't know too. But so what? He gave so much to her that it was worth it.

She smiled as she thought of all the nice things Larry did. Raking her leaves. Shoveling her walk in winter. Making her little trinkets and gifts. He'd even volunteered to come with her to the police station this morning so she wouldn't have to go in alone, though she knew his schedule at the welding shop was very busy.

But where was he? He'd said he'd meet her here. She glanced at her watch. Oh well, she should head in, and he would turn up soon, she was sure.

She got out of her car and straightened her outfit. Making sure to lock the door—one could never be too careful these days—she started across the street.

Movement around the side of the building caught her eye. She glanced over, her heart stopping. Wait... was that...

"Prudence?"

The furry figure sniffing the bush jerked her attention in Barbara's direction. Barbara's eyes locked on those deep-brown pools of adoration, and she fell to her knees. Prudence bounded over and showered her with kisses.

"My little baby!" Barbara picked the dog up and cradled her. "Mommy missed you."

"You found her!"

Barbara had been so focused on her joyous reunion with Prudence that she hadn't noticed Larry arrive. Her heart lifted even further. He hadn't forgotten to meet her after all. Truth was, she had been a little worried about that.

Larry bent down to hug her and accept kisses from the dog. "Did the police find her?"

"No. She was just here."

Larry frowned and turned to look at the street. "Here? How did she get here?"

That was a good question. Had the kidnapper dropped her off? Barbara set Prudence down and inspected her. She seemed fine. She wasn't too thin, her hair was glossy, and she was happily wagging her tail.

Barbara's heart constricted as she looked across the street. "If someone did drop her here, it was totally irresponsible. She could have gotten hit by a car!"

"Well, to be fair, there isn't much traffic here."

"Maybe she escaped from the kidnapper and wandered here?"

"Maybe."

Larry had a funny expression on his face, and Barbara suddenly felt defensive. "I hope you don't think she ran off like others are saying. I'm very careful about not letting her out. And even if she did —which she didn't—how could she have gotten way over here?"

Larry glanced behind the police station. "There is the woods that backs up to your neighborhood…"

Barbara picked Pru up again and stood. "That's almost a mile away! She could never walk that far. No. Someone took her, and it's only by some miracle that she's found her way to me."

Larry smiled indulgently. "That's all that matters. And she looks like she's in good shape. Will you bring her into the station?" He gestured toward the glass doors of the police station a few feet away.

Barbara thought about it. What was the point? "No, I'll just call Detective Perillo and let him know."

"Okay then." Larry put his arm around her and guided her toward her car. "Let's get the two of you home."

Chapter Nineteen

THE POLICE TAPE was gone from the display case at Farraday Jewelers, and Douglas was behind the counter when Nans, Ruth, Ida, and Helen visited the store. It was no coincidence that Douglas was the only one on duty. The ladies had been watching the store for quite some time, waiting for an opportunity to talk to him alone.

"Douglas. How are you?" Nans feigned concern. Truth be told, Douglas didn't look so good. He was sweating, and he had dark circles under his eyes. Guilt keeping him up at night?

"I'm doing pretty good. I mean, all things considered. Having a hard time with the insurance," Douglas said.

"Oh, they always do try to weasel out of paying," Helen said.

Douglas nodded. "What can I help you with?"

Ida fiddled around in her purse, pulled out her cell phone, and squinted at it. They'd arranged ahead of time that she'd feign old-lady-itis, pretending she didn't know how to work the device to cover up that she was really taking a picture of Douglas. They'd take that picture to Jeffrey, and hopefully, he'd be able to identify Douglas as the "grandson" who had brought in the jewelry.

"Well, let me see." Ida brought the phone up to her face and fumbled around with it a bit before pressing the camera button and then acting surprised when the flash went off. "Ooops... Fat fingered it. I was looking for my list. It's on my phone here." She snapped off a few more pictures just for good measure. "There we are. Yes. It's so terrible when you get old and forget things so easily." Ida looked at Douglas, and he nodded sympathetically. "Anyway, a dear friend of ours, Eleanor Robinson, passed away recently, and we've heard her grandson brought her jewelry to a jeweler, and we were wondering if you have it. We'd like to buy some pieces as a memento."

Nans had been watching Douglas carefully to see if there was any look of recognition when Ida mentioned Eleanor Robinson, but he didn't even flinch.

Douglas pressed his lips together and shook his head. "No. We don't have any estate jewelry here. Why don't you try Jeffrey's? He takes that sort of thing in."

"Oh, how disappointing," Nans said. "I guess we'll have to go out that way. How are the police coming along with the investigation?" Nans nodded toward where the diamond display case had been. The case was still there, but now it was filled with rubies and emeralds.

Douglas seemed to deflate. He sat down hard in the chair. "I'm afraid it's not coming so good. You see, I might have messed up."

A confession so soon? Nans couldn't believe her luck. She remembered how she'd seen Douglas at the police station. Perhaps she wasn't the only one that suspected he had something to do with it. But why was he confessing it to her so readily now?

"Messed up? How?" Helen asked to prod him along.

"It was my responsibility to make sure the security system was working properly. But I procrastinated, and by the time I called the security company, Freddy wasn't able to fix it properly because there was a part he needed, and it couldn't be delivered for several days. That's why the camera was still glitching that night."

"Freddy?"

Douglas nodded. "Yes. Freddy Lang. He works for Lowe's Security. Er... worked, I should say."

"Oh dear, poor Freddy," Ruth said. "Now he won't be able to fix it at all."

"I don't think it's any coincidence that Freddy Lang was supposed to fix the security, do you?" Nans asked as they hurried to Ruth's giant Oldsmobile.

Nans piled into the front next to Ruth. She was taking her life in her hands; Ruth wasn't the best driver. If Nans had had a dollar for every curb Ruth had run over, she would be a rich woman. Not to mention the mailboxes she had mowed down. But since Lexy was busy with the dog show and Ruth was the only one of the ladies with a car, she had no choice.

Hopefully, Jack wouldn't give Ruth a ticket for the horrible parking job that was sure to happen when they got to Jeffrey's.

"If it is a coincidence, it's a very strange one. Do you think the two crimes could be related?" Helen asked.

"It's definitely something to check out. And the fact that we couldn't find Eleanor Robinson's obituary does not bode well." Nans whipped out her cell phone and sent a text to Jack about the Freddy connection. "I know Jack doesn't like it when we meddle, but he may not have discovered this little tidbit, and it won't hurt to keep him informed."

"The sooner the killer and thief are caught, the better. Maybe they are even the same person. And I wouldn't be surprised if it's all tied into my K-Cup thefts," Helen said.

Ida scoffed. "I hardly think the person who killed Freddy and stole the diamonds would also steal K-Cups."

"You never know. It could be a serial criminal. And besides, coffee is expensive," Helen said. "We're still on for setting up the surveillance this afternoon, right, Ruth?"

Ruth had her hands glued to the steering wheel at ten and two and was leaning forward, her nose practically pressed into the wheel. "Yep. Mario is going to have his nephew, William, come and help us out."

"Hopefully, he won't bring his knives," Ida mumbled. They'd met William under rather disturbing circumstances when they had been innocently peering into some windows at Mario's house. William had taken them for peeping Toms and chased them away by throwing knives into the windowsill. He'd turned out to be a good kid, but Ida didn't forgive easily.

Helen ignored her and sat back in her seat. "Good. The sooner we find that culprit, the better."

Nans rolled her eyes. Leave it to Helen to prioritize coffee stealing over murder and theft.

Ruth did her usual bad parking job, and they all traipsed into Jeffery's Jewelers.

Jeffrey seemed pleased to see them. "Did you ladies decide on something?"

"Well, no. We want you to look at something. We were wondering if this gentleman is Eleanor Robinson's grandson." Ida held up her cell phone and scrolled through the pictures she'd taken of Douglas.

Jeffrey squinted, his face mere centimeters from the screen. "Nope. Can't say that he is. The fellow was a little bit younger, with a ruddy complexion."

Darn it. But it seemed as if Jeffrey couldn't see very well. Could he be mistaken?

The door opened, and they all turned around to see Jack.

"You're double parked out there, Ruth," Jack said.

"Oh! Sorry. I'll move it right away." Ruth hurried outside.

"Jack! What brings you here?" Nans asked. Apparently her text had spurred Jack into action.

"I think he came here to give Ruth a ticket," Helen said.

Jack glanced out the window. "Not as long as she parks

it properly this time." He grimaced, and they all watched Ruth narrowly miss a streetlight.

Jack turned back from the window. "I'm actually here to talk to Jeffrey about the new estate jewelry he's taken in from this Eleanor Robinson."

Jack glanced at Nans, giving her a slight nod, and she swelled with pride.

Jeffrey frowned. "Lots of people seem interested in that. Is there some problem?"

"I'd like to see the paperwork from that," Jack said. "There is some question as to the validity, and, well, since a diamond robbery just occurred..."

"Surely you don't think I had anything to do with that! Why, Jeffrey's Jewelers has been a prominent member of the community for generations." Jeffrey was practically shaking.

Jack held his hands up. "No, no. I don't think *you* had anything to do with it. I'm more concerned about the person that brought you the jewelry."

Jeffrey went over to the table of papers and pulled out the same ones he'd shown to Nans and handed them to Jack. Jack perused them then asked to see the jewelry.

Jeffrey pointed to the case. "I've sold a lot of the jewelry already, but this is what's left. Why don't you take it to the police station until this is sorted out. If there's been some shady dealings, I wouldn't feel right selling it anyway." Jeffrey pulled out his ring of keys, which jangled together as his hands shook.

"That's very nice of you. Can I help you with that?" Jack took the keys and opened the case.

Meanwhile, outside, Ruth had knocked over a planter full of geraniums and almost hit a Toyota.

"Well, it looks like you're busy here. We've gotta run." Nans hurried out of the store before Ruth could do more damage.

Chapter Twenty

THE COMMUNITY CENTER in the Brook Ridge Falls Retirement village had glass doors in the front and a metal door in the back. The back door led to the back hallway and the storage room where Helen kept the coffee. Helen figured the thief was getting into the building through the back door because no one in their right mind would risk going in the front. The scratches in the paint near the lock seemed to prove her right.

"Thank you so much for helping us with this, William." Mario picked up a screwdriver and handed it to his nephew.

William was up on a ladder, installing a trail camera on the eaves. Helen had wanted a state-of-the-art surveillance system, but on this short notice and with a limited budget, she'd had to settle for the outdated trail camera that William had had in his garage.

William smiled down at his uncle. "It's no problem. I know you can't do things like you used to because of your arthritis. Are you using that poultice that Aunt Millie gave you?"

Mario rubbed his hands together. "I keep forgetting, but it really does help when I use it."

"She's pretty good with herbs," William said. "She gave me some tea concoction for headaches. Works like a charm. All her herbs are local, too. She picks them out in the woods herself, you know. It's too bad that she might not be around for long."

Mario looked concerned. "What do you mean? Is she ill?"

William spoke while he screwed the camera in. "She's fine, but she can't afford her rent. Don't tell anyone I told you. She doesn't want anyone to know. She told me she might have to move to a less expensive area. In fact, I saw her at Jeffrey's Jewelers the other day myself, selling one of those expensive brooches she always used to wear." William shook his head. "It's a shame, because she's so loyal to the Circo Acrobato family, always giving us free herbal concoctions and such. I wish we could take care of her somehow."

Ruth frowned at Mario. "You know, Mario, he has a point. Some of the members of the Circo Acrobato are quite wealthy, while others are suffering. That doesn't seem right to me. Especially when you claim everyone is *family*." Ruth took a step away from Mario.

Mario was quite wealthy. Nans had been to his house, and it was full of expensive antiques.

Mario looked appropriately concerned. "I guess I never thought about it that way. You might have a point, Ruth, but Millie would never take money. It would hurt her pride."

"Never mind that," Helen said. "Are you sure this camera is going to pick up anyone that comes to the door?"

William descended the ladder. "It sure is. It's an older model, but it still works good. It's activated when it senses movement. It will take a picture of whoever—or whatever—comes up to the door."

"How do we get the pictures?" Ida asked.

"Come around in the morning. There's a little card inside the camera. Press the button on the side, and it will slide out. Then you can use this adapter to transfer the pictures to your computer." William reached into his pocket and took out a small adapter.

Helen took it from him.

Ida frowned. "The next day? I was hoping we could catch the culprit red-handed."

William shrugged. "Sorry. This is all I could come up with on short notice."

"It will do the trick," Helen said. "Thank you very much for setting it up."

"No problem. Okay, I guess I'm done. I'll see you all later."

William left, and Ida turned to the rest of them. "So now what?"

"Now," Helen said, glancing up at the camera on the roof's edge, "we wait."

Chapter Twenty-One

"COME ON, Sprinkles. I promise we won't find a body in here this time." Lexy glanced up as she cajoled the dog toward Doggy Diva. It appeared to be business as usual inside. Customers were milling in the lobby, and there was no sign of the police, fortunately.

Lexy opened the door, and Sprinkles sniffed the air as if to assure herself that it was safe to go inside. The air must have passed muster, because after a few sniffs, she trotted in and up to the desk.

Kelly Farmer was at the desk. She looked a lot better than when Lexy had last seen her.

"Hi, Lexy. Hey there, Sprinkles." Kelly came around the desk and crouched to pet the fluffy dog. Sprinkles sat and gave her her paw. "Looks like you need your nails done. Don't worry. We'll fix you up nice and pretty."

Kelly picked Sprinkles up and took the end of the leash from Lexy. "The usual?"

"That would be great," Lexy said. "It's good to see that you're feeling better about being here."

Kelly grimaced. "It took me a little while, and I'm still pretty sad about Freddy, but work has to go on."

"I know. I'm just glad the dogs weren't traumatized. Some dogs are so sensitive, and they seem to know things. I wondered why Sprinkles was hesitant to come in here. And I imagine poor Queenie must've been a nervous wreck."

Kelly frowned. "Queenie? You mean Edwina Southwick's dog?"

Lexy nodded. "Yes. She was here for grooming that morning, right?"

Kelly thought for a while then shook her head. "No. I'm sure Queenie wasn't here. Edwina is a little forgetful, so if she told you that, then maybe she just forgot what day she brought her. In fact, I remember she brought her in the next day, and we were barely getting settled in again."

"Oh, right. You know how it is—the days all run into one. I'll be back this afternoon to pick Sprinkles up," Lexy said.

"Okay. See you then."

Lexy went back to the bakery and spent the rest of the morning catching up on business. There were scones to make, and she still had dozens of dog-shaped cookies to bake for the dog show. Luckily, Cassie had held down the fort and was standing at the stainless steel table, piping strands of frosting onto an oversized dog-shaped cake.

Cassie stood back and looked at the cake. "It's supposed to be a sheepdog."

Lexy could see the resemblance, but it wasn't quite there. "Maybe the frosting needs to be stiffer." It had started to form soft globs.

"Yeah. But the shape is good, right?"

The shape of a dog sitting was pretty good. "Yep."

"Okay. I used a combination of bundt cake pans and layer pans then carved the cake out and stuck the pieces together with frosting. I can repeat that and make the frosting less gooey. I think the Swiss buttercream would be better. Guess your grandma and her henchmen are going to get a lot of free cake." Cassie gestured toward the melting sheepdog.

"Ida will love that."

The oven timer dinged, and Lexy slid the last batch of cookies out. She carefully scraped each one off with a spatula and placed them on the rack to cool. Cassie would frost them later.

"I think I'm caught up." Lexy untied her apron. "Can you handle things while I take one last trip over to the armory? I want to measure the table and then do a mock-up here to make sure we bring the right serving and display stands."

"Of course." Cassie gave her a pointed look. "And I bet you want to get a chance to talk to some of your suspects while you are there, too."

Lexy smiled. "You know me too well. It never hurts to chat it up. Nans taught me never to underestimate the power of clues coming out during normal conversation."

"Leave it to Nans."

Cassie went back to her work, and Lexy pulled a container of finished cookies off the shelf. It wouldn't hurt to bring a few bribes while she was at it.

The armory was buzzing with activity. Anastasia was rushing around, instructing people to move this and rearrange that. Every so often, she'd run out to the audience area to see how things looked from that perspective.

"Lexy! You're back!" Anastasia bustled over and picked a cookie out of the container.

"I wanted to take some last-minute measurements and make sure I bring the right amount of treats to make for a good presentation."

"That's my girl! I knew I could count on you to make things look just perfect. Now, what do you think of the locations of the show rings and grooming stations?" Anastasia gestured toward the rest of the room.

"It looks great." Lexy scanned the room, taking note of all the dog owners with their pets. Her gaze skidded to a stop when she saw Barbara *with* Prudence. "Prudence is here!"

"Yes. Barbara and Prudence were reunited this morning. Isn't it wonderful?"

"It is. Did someone turn Prudence in?" She hadn't talked to Jack yet today, and he couldn't be expected to call her about every little development in his cases.

"Not exactly. Apparently, Barbara was taking Prudence's brush to the police station, and there she was!"

"She was just loose in the street?"

"Yes. Isn't that a lovely coincidence?"

It sure was. Lexy spotted someone frantically waving in Anastasia's direction from the other end of the armory.

"Oh dear. Eduardo needs me for something."

Anastasia ran off, and Lexy headed toward Barbara.

"You got Prudence back!" She reached out and patted the little dog. Prudence really was a cutie with her long, silky hair secured high in a purple bow on top of her head. Her adoring brown eyes stared up at the container of cookies.

"Yes!" Barbara picked the dog up and cuddled her to her chest. "It's like a miracle! I was so worried and afraid we would never find her, but there she was, right in front of the police station."

"How odd. So she really did get out of the house then?" Lexy held the cookie container out to Barbara, who put Pru down on the table and picked one.

"No, I don't think she did. How she ended up at the police station I'll never know. I can only assume that the kidnapper had a change of heart and let her go. Maybe they figured the police would see her and pick her up before anything bad happened." Her gaze narrowed and shifted over to Edwina. "Or maybe they did something to my Prudence to affect her performance in the dog show and *then* let her go."

Lexy glanced over at Edwina, who was cleaning the wrinkles on Queenie's face. The dog, normally jittery and dancing around, looked like she was napping.

"You think someone tampered with poor Pru? What would they do?" Lexy asked.

"I don't know. So far, Prudence seems fine, but what if

they gave her something that would make her hair fall out or make her go to the bathroom in an inopportune moment? I've heard all kinds of shenanigans happen at these shows, and there is more than one person who's vying for the top spot." Barbara's gaze shifted from Edwina to Millie, who was at her table with Winston, putting him through a series of commands.

"Well, I hope not. And I certainly hope no one would do anything that harmed her." Prudence looked to be in good health to Lexy. Her eyes were bright, and she was standing tall, her recently brushed fur silky.

"Let's hope. Larry was there with me, and he checked her out and thinks she seems fine, too."

"That's good." As far as Lexy knew, Larry was no veterinarian. She remembered he was some sort of metal-worker and had once made cute, intricate little boxes for one of the senior center fundraisers.

"Yes. He's very devoted to me and Prudence."

"Well, I'm glad you got her back. I'm just going to take these cookies around and offer them to everyone."

"Thank you. We'll talk later," Barbara said. "And thank your grandmother for taking me down to the police station and Jack for paying so much attention to this issue. I've called to let him know he can close the case."

Lexy was making her way toward Millie when her phone rang. It was Nans.

"Lexy, I need a ride."

Lexy felt a pang of anxiety. "Are you okay?"

"Oh, yes, dear, it's nothing bad. It's just that Ida and Helen are getting their hair done, and Ruth is nowhere to be found." Nans lowered her voice to a whisper. "I think she might be with Mario."

"Okay. And you need to go somewhere right away?"

"Yep. I've made Jack's favorite Reuben sandwich and need to get it to him right away."

"Really? That's kind of out of the blue." What was Nans up to?

"Not really. Gus down at the butcher's had corned beef on sale, so naturally, I bought a good amount. It has to be used up before it goes bad, and I figured what better way than to make Jack a sandwich, since it's his favorite. I made one for myself too. Would you like one?"

"No, thanks." Lexy glanced around. She'd been planning to engage Millie and Edwina in conversation to see if any clues dropped out, but she actually had no idea what to say or what she was looking for. Clearly, Nans had something in mind with this sandwich business, and that might be a lot more interesting and productive.

"Lexy? Are you there? The sandwich is going to get cold, so we'd better hurry."

"Alrighty then. I'm at the armory, finalizing the setup for the dog show. Let me just take some measurements, and then I'll be right over."

Chapter Twenty-Two

THE SMELL of corned beef and sauerkraut permeated every molecule of air in Lexy's small VW Beetle.

Lexy glanced over at her grandmother, who was in the passenger seat with the tinfoil-wrapped sandwich in her lap. "Okay, spill. What's the real reason you want to go to see Jack?"

Nans looked sheepish. "You saw through me that quick?"

"Yep."

Nans sighed. "Fine. We visited Douglas Farraday, and he denied having anything to do with bringing that jewelry to Jeffrey's. But Ida managed to sneak some pictures of him, and we took those over to Jeffrey's to see if he recognized him."

"And did he?"

"No. Douglas isn't the fake grandson. But while we were there, Jack came in. He must have been following up on all the clues we found about the case." Nans sounded pleased as punch.

Lexy's left brow ticked up. "Really? And what happened?"

"Jeffrey was quite upset, as you can imagine. I feel he is totally innocent in this. He gave the jewelry to Jack and said he wouldn't feel right selling it if there was any question as to its legitimacy."

Lexy pulled into a parking spot behind the police station and shifted in her seat to look at Nans. "So you're hoping Jack found out something more about the jewelry then?"

Nans nodded as she opened the door. "Yes. And the other thing too—Douglas did admit one thing. He slacked off with the security. He was supposed to have the security guy in, but he waited too long, and then they needed a part. That's why the camera was still glitchy. And guess who the security guy was."

Lexy frowned. "I have no idea."

"Freddy Lang."

"Whoa. That's an interesting coincidence."

Nans nodded. "And you know what I always say: there's no such thing as a coincidence."

"But what does that mean? The robbery and the murder are related?"

"It could be. Perhaps Freddy knew a bit too much, and that's why he was killed."

"So then all this stuff going on with the dog show, the dognapping, and Edwina's car being seen at Doggy Diva the morning of the murder has nothing to do with the prize for the dog show. That would make sense, because the prize isn't big enough to be a motive for murder."

Nans frowned. "Edwina's car was at Doggy Diva?"

"Yeah. I guess we haven't had a chance to catch up today. Jack told me last night that one of the surveillance cameras on the street showed Edwina's car at Doggy Diva early that morning. And there's another development I bet you don't know about either." Usually, Nans knew everything, so Lexy loved having the rare opportunity to get the scoop first.

Nans looked doubtful. "What's that?"

"Prudence has been returned to Barbara."

Nans was surprised. "You don't say! When? How?"

Lexy told her about Barbara finding the dog as they walked over to the police station.

"Sounds very convenient to me," Nans said.

Anita Dugan was sitting at the desk. She sniffed the air, her nose twitching a few times. She turned and yelled, "Jack, you got one of those smelly sandwich deliveries from your grandmother-in-law."

Jack popped his head out of the office. His face split into a smile when he saw them, but then his expression turned suspicious. "How nice of you to stop by unannounced. Come on back." Jack kissed Lexy on the forehead and took the sandwich from Nans then settled back behind his desk. "This is really nice of you, Mona. I'm starving."

"Well, I like to do what I can." Nans walked slowly around the room, her gaze scanning the whiteboard, the papers on Jack's desk, the computer screen.

Lexy didn't think she was being very subtle about it,

and apparently, neither did Jack, judging by the amused expression on his face as he tried to stop sauerkraut from dripping all over the desk.

"Are you looking for something in particular, Mona?" He wiped his chin.

Nans managed to look shocked. "Me? No. I'm just keeping things circulating. When you get to be my age, it's good to always keep moving."

"I just came from the dog show," Lexy said. "I was glad to see that Prudence has been found."

Jack nodded, pausing to chew a big bite of sandwich. "Barbara called me. Said the dog was in good condition."

"Don't you think it's a little odd she just randomly showed up?" Nans asked.

Jack shrugged. "If the dog ran off out of the house, she could have been wandering around for a few days. Dogs are known to do that, right?"

"I don't know. It's pretty far from here to the retirement village," Nans said. "It took Lexy and me a good ten minutes to drive here by car."

"Sure, driving-wise," Jack said. "But don't forget the forest backs up from her yard to right behind the station. If Prudence got out of the house somehow, she'd probably wander into the forest, and she might have cut right across and ended up out on the street here. Anyway, it's great that she was found safe. Especially since it seems like there may be something going on in that forest."

That got Nans's attention. "What do you mean, something going on?"

Jack leaned back in his chair, smiling. Of course Nans

thought he was letting something slip, but Lexy could tell he was giving out the information on purpose. Sometimes, Jack threw Nans a bone because he knew that as a harmless senior citizen, she could get information out of people who might not want to talk to the police.

"You know the jewelry I got from Jeffrey's earlier this morning?"

"Yes. We were happy to help give you that lead," Nans said.

"Right. Well, we ran it through our test that shows trace elements found on the item."

"Yes, I believe you mentioned you could do that before."

"We found something very interesting. Apparently, the diamonds in the jewelry have been in the forest."

"In the forest?"

Jack nodded. "As you know, we have a huge population of deer here, and oddly enough, we found residue from deer antlers on the diamonds."

"But why would the diamonds be in the forest?" Nans asked.

"Who knows? Maybe the thief thought it was a good place to hide them. If someone stole them from Farraday Jewelers and wanted to stash them somewhere until they could put them in those settings, that might be an ideal place," Jack said.

"How do you know the diamonds in the jewelry were from Farraday's though?"

"I don't think the thief was very smart. Diamonds have tiny identification numbers etched into them. You need a special magnifier to read them, but Louise came in today and identified them."

"You don't say. That is an interesting twist." Nans looked at Lexy. "Well, I think I better get back to my place. Helen is coming over later with the big reveal from the trail camera, and I need to get a little nap in. You're invited to join us, Lexy." Nans turned to Jack. "Hope you enjoyed the sandwich."

"I did. And the company, as always." Jack winked at Lexy as she followed Nans out of his office.

Lexy knew better than to show up for a session with the Ladies' Detective Club empty-handed, so she made sure to snag some treats from the Cup and Cake before going over to Nans's place to look at the trail camera photos later that day. Cassie had cut the failed sheepdog cake into pieces, which were perfect to bring for the ladies.

Ida took the box from her as soon as she stepped through the door.

"I'll just get these out on some dessert plates." She bustled away into the kitchen.

"I just finished filling everyone in on our little visit with Jack," Nans said.

"Interesting developments, but I'm really glad that Prudence is okay," Ruth said. She was sitting at the dining room table, fiddling with a brown rectangular device that Lexy assumed was the trail camera.

"Do you have that card out yet?" Ida asked as she slid the refreshments onto the table.

"I'm not sure which button to press." Ruth started shaking the box and pressing various buttons until finally, a thin card slid out. She handed it to Helen, who fitted it into the adapter.

"Now, if I just attach this to my computer..." Ruth picked up her iPad and started looking at the edges for a slot that matched the one on the adapter.

"I don't think you can put that in an iPad," Lexy said. "I think you need a computer."

"I have one in the office." Nans headed off down the hall, returning quickly with a laptop.

Helen squinted at the sides of it and finally found the right slot.

A window appeared on the computer, showing a grainy black-and-white picture of a raccoon approaching a trashcan outside the senior center.

"That doesn't look like our thief," Nans said. "Try clicking on the arrow."

Helen did as told and scrolled through a picture of a deer, a cat, and a blurry image of a couple.

Ida squinted, almost pressing her nose against the screen. "Hey, that looks like Ruth and Mario."

Everyone turned to face Ruth, whose cheeks turned bright red. "I was helping him with the accounting. He is the treasurer, you know, and he can hardly press the buttons on the calculator with his arthritis."

Nans looked incredulous. "In the middle of the night?"

"It looks like you're kissing," Ida said.

Ruth grabbed the computer. "Never mind that. Let's see if we can find the thief." She clicked the arrow several times.

"Stop. I thought I saw something." Lexy reached around Ruth and hit the back arrow. Everyone gasped.

The picture on the screen was of Millie Dixon. She had her head bent over the lock to the storeroom. The next frame showed her opening the door.

"Looks like we found our K-Cup thief!" Helen's tone was triumphant.

Nans's eyes narrowed. "Millie Dixon? Millie was in the woods, gathering herbs. Jack thinks the diamonds were in the woods. William saw her at Jeffrey's Jewelers. Maybe stealing K-Cups isn't her only crime."

Chapter Twenty-Three

MILLIE DIXON LIVED in a small ranch-style house in the older section of the retirement village. She was out in the side yard, hanging herbs to dry, when they pulled up in Ruth's Oldsmobile. Ruth screeched to a stop, narrowly missing Millie's mailbox.

Millie looked appropriately dismayed to see them all descending on her. Winston did too. He positioned himself between Millie and the ladies, assessing them with watchful eyes.

"There's no use pretending you're innocent. We've caught you red-handed!" Helen held up the picture they'd printed from the trail camera.

Millie seemed unfazed. "What are you talking about?"

Helen fisted her hands on her hips. "Don't you play dumb with me. I'm talking about the K-Cups. You've been stealing them from the community center!"

Millie grimaced. Winston growled at Helen.

Millie bent down to pet the dog. "Be nice, Winston. These are friends."

Winston stopped growling, but he still eyed Helen warily, apparently unconvinced by Millie's words.

Nans eyed the herbs. "And maybe not just the K-Cups. Maybe the diamonds too."

"Diamonds? I don't know anything about diamonds. And I didn't *steal* the K-Cups. I just borrowed them."

"Aha! You heard her, girls. She's confessed!" Ida said.

Millie held her hands up. "Not so fast. I said I borrowed them. I ran a bit short on funds, and, well... A girl must have her coffee. But I think if you look, you'll discover that nothing has actually been stolen, because I replaced everything I took."

Ida made a face. "What are you talking about? We have you right here in black and white." Ida tapped the picture. "It shows you breaking into the community center."

Millie crossed her arms over her chest. "That might be so, but I think if you go and look at your inventory, you'll see there are actually extra K-Cups. As I said, I only borrowed some, and last night, I was merely returning what I borrowed."

Helen narrowed her eyes at Millie. "So you say. I'm going to call your bluff."

They all hurried to the senior center, which was just a few streets over. Nans didn't think Millie was bluffing. Why would she? But if Millie was a thief with a conscience who only borrowed things and then returned them, that blew a hole in her diamond theory.

The senior center wasn't being used, so all the doors

were locked. Helen unlocked the door to the storage room and flung it open, rushing over to the shelf that held the K-Cups. She whipped out the tray on which they were stored, her face going from triumph to confusion. "What? There's more K-Cups in here than there were yesterday."

"See. I told you," Millie said.

Winston yipped his agreement.

"Oh, and by the way, you should find a better supplier. The batch I got the other day tasted like dandelions. Yech." Millie made a bitter-lemon face.

"I put dandelion tea in them. I thought the thief would complain, and I could catch them that way," Helen said.

"It was a pretty good plan. But Millie never complained," Ida said.

"Who complains about something they stole... err... borrowed?" Millie asked. "I'm smarter than that."

Millie was pretty smart, but was she smart enough to be lying about this? Why though? It didn't make any sense that she'd returned the K-Cups before she knew they suspected her.

"So you didn't have anything to do with the diamond heist?" Ruth asked.

"Of course not. If I did, do you think I'd be stealing K-Cups? I'd have plenty of money for coffee."

She had a point.

"But you just returned some, so you must have come into money," Nans pointed out.

"I wish. I actually had to sell some of my precious antique brooches. Jeffrey was very nice to take them." Millie sniffed.

That explained why William had seen her at Jeffrey's Jewelers, but Nans wasn't ready to let her off the hook for everything just yet.

"And what about Prudence? Did you have something to do with kidnapping her?" Nans asked.

That made sense, because Barbara had mentioned that she was afraid someone had given Prudence something that might affect her performance at the dog show, and Millie was an expert on herbs. With Prudence out of the way, Winston stood a better chance at winning.

"Of course not! I'm not some kind of monster. I'm a dog lover." She scooped up Winston and cuddled him in her arms. "But I do know someone who might be involved."

"Who's that?" Nans asked.

"Edwina Southwick. She wants to win the dog show badly. I happened to overhear her and Carl Newtson talking when they thought no one could hear them, and it sounded like the two of them were up to something."

Millie seemed hesitant to give more details, but Nans got the feeling she had more.

"I saw her and Carl whispering suspiciously at the armory when I was setting up for the dog show, and Carl was acting very strange the morning Freddy was killed," Lexy said.

"But surely you don't think they had something to do with what happened to Freddy?" Ruth said.

"I don't know about that. But have you noticed Queenie has been acting very serene lately?" Millie asked Lexy.

"I did notice that. She's usually so hyper, and I heard that's the reason Queenie never wins."

"Right. Well, Barbara wasn't wrong about people giving something to a dog that could cause them to act differently. In fact, there are several herbs one can give that might influence their behavior. Like perhaps turning a hyper dog into a more sedate dog."

"You think Edwina might be giving something to Queenie? But so what? Is that illegal?"

"Depends on what she's giving her." Millie seemed to mull something over, then she sighed. "When I was out collecting my herbs in the forest, I noticed something was amiss. There is a very rare herb, indigo nightroot, that grows in the woods behind Barbara's house. It's on the endangered list, and when I was out collecting herbs the other day, I noticed that those plants had been pulled up."

"Pulled up? Like by a person?" Nans asked.

"At first, I thought an animal had dug them up," Millie said. "But then when I inspected further, I saw a footprint. A big boot. And then when I was at the armory, I just happened to notice that Carl was wearing big boots."

"What would happen to someone if they took the herbs?" Nans asked.

"Endangered plants?" Ruth cut in. "You would get a big fine and possibly jail time for digging them up."

"What if Edwina and Carl were up to something with these herbs and Freddy found out? Edwina's car was seen at Doggy Diva the morning of his murder."

"I wouldn't put it past Carl to be selling the herbs. He's kind of shady," Lexy said.

"That's terrible!" Ruth exclaimed. "Are these herbs dangerous? I can't believe Edwina would endanger her dog just to win a dog show."

"They can be dangerous, even fatal... but what if Edwina doesn't know that?" Millie asked. "Carl might have sold them to her and not told her of the dangers."

"But if Edwina is giving Queenie the herbs, then why kidnap Prudence?" Nans asked.

"That's a good question," Helen said.

"There's only one way to find out. Edwina lives the next street over. I say we pay her a visit," Nans suggested.

"Good idea," Millie said. "I'll go with you. I think we better swing by my place and pick up some antidote herbs. If Edwina doesn't know the right dosage for Queenie, I have a feeling we might need them."

Chapter Twenty-Four

EDWINA LIVED in a charming cottage on Ivy Lane. She'd reluctantly invited them inside, and they now sat on overstuffed sofas and chairs in her living room. The room was small but had large, bright windows and a brick fireplace. Doilies covered the end tables. Edwina hadn't offered them any coffee or tea, and Nans could see that Ida was a bit disappointed with that. She didn't have time for niceties though. She had a killer to catch.

"Really, Mona, I don't see what you're getting at." Edwina Southwick made a face to indicate she was appropriately offended by Nans's insinuation that she had done something shady. She had a lethargic Queenie in her lap and seemed distracted and concerned as she petted the little pug's ears.

"We know that you're up to something," Nans said. "And I have it on good authority that your car was parked at Doggy Diva the morning Freddy Lang was killed."

Edwina gasped and covered Queenie's ears. "Mona Baker, are you accusing me of murder?"

Nans shrugged. "If the shoe fits…"

"Well, the shoe doesn't fit."

Queenie snorted, and Edwina jerked her attention back to the little dog. "Oh, you're waking up from your nap. That's a good girl." She patted Queenie, and when she got no further response, she shook her a little roughly, but the dog didn't stir.

"I've never seen Queenie so sleepy." Millie sidled closer to the dog, bending down to look at her face. "Are you sure she's not ill?"

Edwina moved Queenie to face away from Millie. "She's not ill. She's just tired. All those dog-show activities take a lot out of her."

"I'll bet," Ida said.

Edwina gave her a sharp look. "Now, I'd appreciate it if you people would leave. You're upsetting her."

Apparently, Edwina didn't know that one couldn't get rid of Nans that easily. "I think we still have some things to talk about. What was your car doing at Doggy Diva that day?"

Millie circled to the other side of Edwina and crouched in front of Queenie's face.

"And don't say you were dropping Queenie off for grooming. We checked, and you weren't," Ruth said.

"And Lexy saw you acting suspiciously with Carl Newtson at the dog show. What gives there?" Ida asked.

Edwina waved her hand dismissively. "Suspicious? Hardly. We were simply discussing strategy."

With Edwina distracted by the questioning, Millie reached over and peeled up Queenie's eyelid. "Aha! Just as I thought. Her pupils are dilated."

Edwina's attention swiveled to Millie. "Dilated? What does that mean? Get your hands off my dog!" She jerked Queenie away.

Millie stood and fisted her hands on her hips. "Edwina Southwick, now, you listen to me. I know you don't want to harm Queenie, but if you have given her something, I suggest you tell us, because certain herbs can be very harmful to dogs, and Queenie is showing the signs of a dog that has ingested something very bad. Maybe even something fatal."

Edwina looked suitably alarmed. "Fatal?"

Millie pursed her lips and nodded.

Edwina's expression turned skeptical. "I don't believe you. Carl said it would only..." Her eyes widened, and she slapped her hand over her mouth.

"Aha! So you did give her something!" Millie said.

"And you and Carl *are* involved in shenanigans," Nans added.

Edwina looked conflicted. Her gaze traveled from Millie to Nans to Queenie. She gave the dog a shake, but Queenie just let out a sigh. "Okay! I admit it. I bought some herbs from Carl. He said they would calm her down for the dog show, and he told me not to tell anyone because it was illegal!" She turned imploring eyes on Millie. "Can you help her?"

Millie rummaged in her basket, pulling out some herbs and a vial of something green. She rushed over to Queenie and waved the vial under her nose. After a few seconds, the dog sputtered. "Good girl."

"Will she be okay?" Edwina was practically frantic.

Millie dabbed some of the liquid from the vial on Queenie's lips. Her pink tongue darted out. Then Millie crumbled some dried herbs and sprinkled them on Queenie's tongue. The pug lapped the herbs. Then she snorted, her feet jerked, and her eyes sprang open.

"Just as I thought. You've given her indigo nightroot. It could have killed her, but I think she will be okay now. She's eating the antidote." Millie looked at Edwina sharply. "You should never ever give herbs to your dog like that."

Edwina was in tears. "I'm so sorry. I just wanted to win, and Carl said this would help."

Queenie moved around in Edwina's lap, and Millie gave her more herbs. As they watched, the dog became more lively and then looked up at Edwina and licked her face.

"Thank goodness she's okay!" Edwina exclaimed.

"I'm glad she's okay," Nans said. "But I'm afraid I'm going to have to call Jack and have you arrested for murder."

"Murder!" Edwina was shocked.

"Yep. I know exactly what happened. You just admitted that you got the herbs from Carl and that it's illegal to have them," Nans said.

"So how does that make me a murderer?" Edwina asked.

"I think Freddy Lang found out what you two were up to. Maybe he confronted you that day. Your car was seen outside, but Queenie wasn't there for grooming. I think you did bring her, but when you killed Freddy—either by accident or on purpose—you didn't want to leave her there as evidence, so you took her home. Unfortunately, you couldn't get the leash out of Freddy's hands, so you had to leave it there!"

"What? I never even saw Freddy Lang that morning." Edwina dodged kisses from Queenie.

"Aha! So you admit you were there," Ida said.

Edwina frowned. "Okay, I was there. I was meeting Carl to get the herbs, and we met very early, before anyone was out, because we didn't want to be seen. I never saw Freddy. The shop wasn't even open yet, and I certainly didn't have Queenie there, nor did I leave her leash behind."

Lexy glanced at Nans. Jack had said that Edwina's car was there early on the morning of the murder. She could be telling the truth. But there was one thing that didn't make sense. "You and Carl were whispering together at the dog show, and he was acting so jittery the morning of the murder. I remember he ran into his office and then claimed his security camera was a dummy, but I don't think Jack quite believed him. Now, if you and he killed Freddy, maybe he tampered with the cameras on purpose so the police wouldn't see the murder."

Edwina shook her head violently. "No. That's not why. Yes, we were whispering, of course, because we didn't want anyone to know about the herbs. And Carl did tamper with the security files on purpose. But not because of Freddy; because they would have recorded our transaction in the lobby. But in doing so, he had to erase the footage that would have shown Freddy's murder too."

"So he saw who murdered Freddy?" Nans was incredulous.

"Unfortunately, he didn't. He's not very good at figuring out technology, and the police were right outside the room, so he erased everything without looking at it." Edwina stopped and thought a minute. "Or at least that's what he told me."

"Sure," Nans said. "Well, you can tell that to Jack, and we'll see what he thinks."

"Wait! Don't call the police. It wasn't me, I swear. I heard Freddy died right after Doggy Diva opened at ten that day, isn't that right?"

"Yes..."

"And you know it takes ten minutes to get from here to there, right?"

"Yeees..." Nans drew the word out.

"Well then, I have an alibi!"

"What? Who?"

"Larry Morrison. I ran into him that very morning when I was walking Queenie. He was walking Prudence and had stopped to pick up some poop, and I told him he could throw it in my trash. But he's such a nice boy, he said he could never do that and would take it home to dispose of. I know what time it was because I was walking Queenie right before we went to the armory to check out the dog-show setup, and you can verify that I arrived there promptly at ten-fifteen," Edwina said.

Nans frowned. If what Edwina had said was true, she

wouldn't have had time to kill Freddy, walk Queenie, and get to the armory by ten-fifteen. But was it true? Would Larry remember the time?

There was no way she could call Jack unless she had solid proof. She'd have to talk to Larry first, because she didn't want Jack to lose faith in her skills if she tipped him off to the wrong suspect. Not to mention she didn't want to accuse the wrong person of murder.

But murder wasn't the only thing she was investigating. What about the kidnapping of Prudence and the theft of the diamonds? Could Edwina be mixed up in either of those?

"Okay, gang, we're going to check out this alibi. Barbara only lives one street over, and she can call Larry. We'll see if what you say is true." Nans started out of the house, turning back to Edwina. "Don't you go anywhere. We'll be back."

Chapter Twenty-Five

MILLIE VEERED off to her house on the way to Barbara's, and Nans, Lexy, and the ladies continued on.

As they marched up the walkway toward Barbara's front door, Ida tapped Nans on the shoulder. "I don't know, Mona. I'm not so sure about this. Something is off."

Nans turned to look at her. "What do you mean?"

"I think Edwina might be lying. I was calculating the time frame in my head, and I don't think she could have run into Larry walking Prudence the morning Freddy was killed."

Helen nodded. "Ida's right. Remember, Barbara said that Prudence had been kidnapped early that morning while she was out shopping. But if that were the case, then Larry couldn't have been walking her when Edwina claims to have seen him."

Nans pressed her lips together. "That's a good point. But is Edwina lying, or is Barbara lying?"

Ida's brows shot up. "Ohhh... good question."

Barbara's front door opened, and she stepped out, stopping abruptly as she noticed the gathering on her doorstep. "Oh. Mona, what are you all doing here? Did you hear Prudence has been returned. All is well."

As if knowing they were talking about her, Prudence trotted out, wagging her tail.

"Lexy told us. That's wonderful." Ruth bent down to pet the dog.

"Did you ever find out where she was?" Nans asked.

"No. The police seemed to lose interest once we found her, but I swear I did not let her out. Someone took her."

"And then just let her go?" Ida cocked her head to look the dog over. "She seems fine."

"She does. I haven't noticed anything unusual about her. I was worried. Maybe she managed to get away before the kidnapper could harm her," Barbara said.

"Perhaps." Nans bent and scratched the little dog behind the ears. She was charming, and Nans was glad that she had not been harmed. "Will you still show her in the dog show?"

Barbara smiled. "Yes. Edwina and Millie are not very happy about that, of course."

"Speaking of Edwina, we were wondering about something she told us earlier. She said that she saw Larry walking Prudence the morning of Freddy Lang's murder."

Barbara frowned. "So?"

"That's the day Prudence disappeared," Ida pointed out.

"Oh! Right. Well, clearly, she must be lying. Probably trying to cover up for the fact that she was the one who stole Prudence... or killed Freddy ... or both," Barbara said.

Nans remained silent.

Barbara frowned. "What? You think *I'm* the one who's lying? I'm not, and I can prove it. Follow me!"

Barbara spun on her heel and stormed back inside, gesturing for them to follow. They followed her into the kitchen.

She picked a bag up off the counter. "Here. As I told you previously, that morning, I had gone to the mall to get ribbons for Prudence's hair. The ones I like are only sold at the Pet Emporium, so I make a special trip every month. Everyone knows that, so clearly, the kidnapper took advantage of my schedule to grab Prudence. As you can see, the time-stamped receipt is in the bag."

Nans opened the bag and checked the receipt, which verified that Barbara had been almost forty minutes away during Freddy Lang's death.

"See? I'm the victim here," Barbara said.

As Nans put the bag down, she noticed a bottle of pet supplements and remembered that Barbara had mentioned that she gave them to Prudence.

Of course! Why hadn't she thought of that sooner? She reached for them, knocking a magnet off the counter. It rolled onto the floor.

"Prudence, no!" Barbara lunged for the dog, who had gone after the item. "Naughty, naughty. You don't want to have another visit to the vet, now, do you?"

Prudence yipped in alarm at the mention of the vet.

"Honestly, the little darling will eat just about

anything," Barbara said as she scooped the magnet out of Pru's reach.

The wheels were turning in Nans's brain as she read the label on the supplements. But before she could speak her hypothesis out loud, a car pulled up in front of the house.

Ida peeked out the window. "Isn't that your car, Barbara?"

"Yes. Larry borrowed it."

Nans's brows rose. "He did? Does he borrow it often?"

"Yes. His old car broke down a lot, but luckily, he just bought a brand-new car. He just hasn't picked it up yet."

Nans nodded. It was all starting to make perfect sense.

"Well, you better confess before he comes in. You don't want your grandson to hear that you did anything nefarious, do you?" Ruth said.

"Ruth, I don't think Barbara did anything," Nans said.

"Gram!" a voice called out from the living room, then Larry appeared in the kitchen doorway. "Oh. Hi." Larry stopped in the doorway, his gaze skittering between Barbara and the others. "I didn't know you had company. I'll come back later."

He started to back out, but Nans stopped him. "No need to leave. Why don't you stay, Larry? In fact, we were coming to see you."

Barbara frowned. "You were?"

Nans nodded sagely. "Larry, when was the last time you borrowed your grandmother's car?"

Larry laughed. "How would I remember that? I don't keep track of the days. Do you, Gram?"

Barbara went to stand next to Larry, who had picked up Prudence and was cuddling her.

"No." She shot Nans an unfriendly look; clearly, she didn't like her accusing Larry.

Nans was unaffected by the nasty look. "Your grandmother tells us you're getting a new car. That must be nice. Did you get a raise at work?"

Larry scowled. "No—"

"That's really none of your business, Mona," Barbara cut in.

"You're right, it isn't. But when it comes to crime, sometimes people have to ask questions that aren't their business."

Barbara stepped in front of Larry. "Are you accusing Larry now? First me, then my grandson."

"I do believe I am. It all makes sense. He was friends with Freddy. Freddy knew how to get around the security for Farraday Jewelers. But Freddy didn't pull off that diamond heist alone, did he?" Nans directed the question at Larry.

Larry scoffed. "I have no idea what you're talking about." He turned to his grandmother. "I think your friend is batty."

"So do I," Barbara said.

"Do you?" Nans glanced out the window at the Jeep. She could see the bumper, which bore several dents. "Because I think you know exactly what I'm talking about. You saw the pictures from the surveillance camera of the robbery at the jewelry store on Jack's board when we were at the police station to report Prudence was missing, didn't you?"

Barbara made a face. "I was much too upset about Prudence to look at any pictures."

"Uh-huh. Well, one of those pictures was the bumper of a car seen in the back lot at Farraday Jewelers the night of the robbery. The camera was angled such that it only caught the bumper, but the bumper had a very distinctive dent in it." Nans paused for effect.

"Oh!" Ida said. "That's why she ran into that sign. She was covering up the dent with a bigger dent. I thought there was something odd about that."

"So Barbara stole the diamonds?" Ruth asked.

Nans shook her head. "Not Barbara. Larry. Larry *and* Freddy. They used Barbara's car, though."

"I don't know what you ladies are talking about," Larry said.

"My Larry is a good boy," Barbara added.

Nans pulled out her cell phone and held it up in front of her. "Right. Well then, Larry won't mind if I take a picture of him and take it down to Jeffrey's Jewelers to see if Jeffrey recognizes him."

The worried look on Larry's face told Nans everything she needed to know. "So what happened, Larry? Did Freddy try to cut you out of the deal, and you killed him? Or did you have a falling out over something else?"

"Now, Mona Baker, you cannot accuse my grandson. He didn't do anything." Barbara wagged her finger in Nans's face.

"Really? Then why did he kidnap Prudence?"

Barbara gasped and turned to look at Larry. "He would never do such a thing, right?"

"Well ..." Larry sputtered.

Barbara stepped away from her grandson. "Larry Everett Morrison, you didn't have anything to do with Prudence's kidnapping, did you?"

Larry hung his head. "I can't lie to you, Gram."

Barbara's mouth opened and closed, but no sound came out. Nans felt sorry for her.

"So you're admitting that you kidnapped Prudence?" Ruth asked.

Larry remained silent, his head hanging.

"Answer her!" Barbara slapped his arm.

"I did," Larry said.

"But why?" Barbara asked in a small voice full of disappointment.

"I think I know." Nans held up the supplement bottle. "Prudence has a bad habit of eating things that fall on the floor, right?"

"Yes. Very costly vet bills, not to mention it's bad for her health and stressful for me," Barbara said.

"My guess is that Larry must have been over here when you weren't home. Maybe he was watching Prudence or just stopped by. Anyway, some of the diamonds fell on the floor, and she ate them." Nans turned to Larry. "Isn't that right, Larry?"

Larry nodded.

"Freddy must've found out and been displeased, and he took Prudence, didn't he?"

Larry's face darkened. "He said I couldn't be trusted! And I couldn't let him take Prudence away."

"So you followed him to Doggy Diva. Was he going to keep Prudence there until the diamonds came out?"

"Yes! But I wasn't going to let him keep her. We had a fight and... Well, I pushed him hard. He hit his head on the edge of the counter. I didn't mean to kill him, but I was angry. He'd grabbed Prudence without a leash. He must have gotten one from the display, and he was clutching it in his hand and wouldn't let go, so I unhooked it from Prudence's collar, grabbed another leash from the display, and took her." Larry was practically in tears.

Larry turned to Barbara, who looked disgusted with him now. "I wouldn't harm her. I just wanted to keep her until she did her business so I could get the diamonds."

"And that's when you ran into Edwina," Helen said.

Larry nodded. "Right after that, I brought her out to do her business here. But I guess the diamonds hadn't had time to make their way through yet, so I had to take her back to my place."

"And once you got the diamonds, you set them into pieces of jewelry and brought them to Jeffrey's Jewelers, pretending you were the grandson of Eleanor Robinson." Nans remembered the lovely bejeweled trinket boxes Larry had made for one of their charity sales at the senior center. He certainly had the skills to set the diamonds into jewelry.

"That was the plan Freddy and I had all along. We figured if we set them into pieces of jewelry, no one would think to see if they were the stolen diamonds. And Jeffrey is so old, well, we figured he wouldn't look into our story."

"You ought to be ashamed of yourself!" Barbara stepped away from Larry, who did look suitably ashamed. "And you just let Prudence go in the street? She could have been killed!"

"No! I didn't just let her go. When you said you were bringing her brush to the police station, I knew I had to get her back to you in case the police matched her hair to that on the leash that Freddy had been holding. She'd already passed the diamonds, and it was the perfect way to return her without getting caught. So I arranged to meet you there, and I showed up ahead of time. When you crossed the street, I just nudged her out from behind the building, and she ran to you. No harm done."

"No harm done? Plenty of harm has been done. I can't believe you caused me that anguish. And I ruined my bumper for you!" Barbara blurted.

"So you *did* have a suspicion that Larry might be involved," Nans said.

Now it was Barbara's turned to look ashamed. "When you said you had heard my car in the middle of the night, I thought maybe Larry had needed to borrow it and didn't want to wake me. I take sleeping pills, and it's hard to get me up, and he knows I don't mind if he just comes and takes it. When I saw the picture of the bumper at the police station, my first instinct was to protect Larry. The only thing I could think of was to make a bigger dent to cover it up."

Nans nodded. "That was actually very clever."

Barbara looked more embarrassed than ever. "But how did you figure out that Prudence had eaten the diamonds?"

Nans tapped the supplements. "I remembered you'd told us that you kept Prudence in tip-top shape with these supplements that have green-lipped mussel and antler velvet. Jack's analysis showed antler cells on the diamonds. We all thought they had been in the woods, but that wasn't the case. They'd picked up the antler velvet residue from being inside Prudence!"

"Very clever, Mona," Ida said.

Nans smiled. "And now, I'm afraid we're going to have to call the police on Larry."

"Oh, no, you're not!" Barbara said.

"Barbara, we have to. It's all out in the open now. I hope you won't resist." Would Barbara and Larry be a match for them? Larry was younger and stronger, but Lexy was young too, and they outnumbered Barbara and Larry by more than two to one.

"Oh, I'm not going to resist. I'm going to call the police myself." Barbara took her phone from the counter and turned sad eyes on Larry. "Larry, I'm sorry I have to do this, but what you did is inexcusable, and this time, I can't cover for you."

Chapter Twenty-Six

THE ARMORY WAS PACKED for the dog show. Primped and fluffed pooches sat at tables, being judged on posture, health, and temperament. Others were trotting around rings and running agility courses.

Lexy stood behind the dessert table and watched the festivities. Her pastries had been a big hit, and the sheepdog cake Cassie had made while Lexy had been confronting the suspects had come out perfectly.

"The American buttercream is my favorite," Nans said as she bit into a cupcake loaded with frosting.

"I like the Swiss." Ida dragged her finger through the frosting on her piece of cake and then popped it into her mouth. "So smooth and creamy."

"No. The French is definitely the best. It's so custardy and not overly sweet," Ruth said as she chowed down on her second chocolate cupcake.

Nans finished her cupcake and patted her lips with a

napkin. "Has Jack given you any more details about the cases?"

"We should be getting a commendation for solving those," Ida said.

"Yeah, three cases in one fell swoop!" Helen added.

Lexy smiled. She doubted Jack was going to hand out commendations. "Jack did say he appreciated the help, but he was about to solve the cases himself anyway."

Ruth scoffed. "Oh, sure, he always says that."

Lexy continued, "Larry did confess to the murder, diamond theft, and dognapping and is cooperating. They found the other missing leash at his apartment."

"He already confessed to us. They could really save the taxpayers a lot of money if they just sent us out on cases," Helen said.

"Did Farraday's get to keep the diamonds that were found at Jeffrey's?" Ida asked.

"Yes, and Larry had to give back the money he got from Jeffrey's Jewelers for the items that were sold," Lexy said.

Helen frowned. "But what about the jewelry that people already purchased? Remember, some of the gals had bracelets at the morning coffee event."

"Jeffrey is contacting them and offering money back or a nicer item in exchange."

"Oh, that is so nice of him. I know he's getting the money back from Larry, but still, it's quite an effort on his part," Helen said.

"He's an honest man." Ida grabbed another cookie. "He didn't have to turn over his customer names, you know."

Ruth glanced at Ida. "Sounds like someone is smitten."

"What? No, I was just saying..." Ida paused. "You're just saying that to deflect attention from your little romance with Mario."

The two women stared at each other, and Nans broke the silence. "Poor Barbara. It must have been hard for her to turn her grandson in."

"Yeah, she doted on him." Ida bit into her cookie. "I guess Edwina pulled out of the dog show."

"She felt terrible about the way she acted. Said nothing was more important than Queenie's health," Helen said.

"Hey, what happened to Carl? He dug up those herbs. I hope Jack throws the book at him." Ida looked at Lexy.

"He's getting a big fine."

"No jail time?" Ida looked disappointed.

"Afraid not." Lexy started rearranging the table. A lot of the items had been purchased, and she didn't want any bare spots.

"Go figure." Ida returned her attention to the dog show going on around them. "Looks like it's down to Prudence and Winston for the top prize."

"I'm rooting for Winston," Helen said. "Millie can use the money more than Barbara."

"Even though Millie was the K-Cup thief?" Ruth asked.

"Technically, she only borrowed them. Barbara, on the other hand, tried to cover up what Larry did."

"But in the end, she did the right thing," Nans said.

Ida waved her hand at them. "Shhh.... Anastasia is doing the final judging."

Everyone looked out into the arena. Prudence and Winston were in the middle of the arena, standing at attention. Millie and Barbara were there too, eyeing each other warily.

Anastasia stood back, turning her head this way and that to study the dogs. She gave a signal, and Barbara took Prudence for a walk around the ring. Prudence's silky fur cascaded down to her feet, where it swept out slightly as she trotted along. The bow on top of her head held a clump of hair that sprayed out like a fountain.

Barbara returned to her original spot, and Anastasia signaled again, this time for Winston. Millie and Winston trotted around. The dog's large ears were perked at attention, his little legs doing double time.

Anastasia walked around to study the dogs from the front. She leaned back and scratched her chin then nodded and walked over to the table to grab the blue ribbon.

Lexy felt as nervous as if she was in the running. The thought of getting Sprinkles to stand still or trot nicely like Winston and Prudence almost made her laugh out loud.

Anastasia returned to stand in front of Barbara, Millie, Prudence, and Winston. "And the winner is...."

Lexy held her breath.

"Prudence Morrison!"

The crowd applauded as Barbara picked Prudence up and gave her a kiss. Anastasia handed over the ribbon. Millie walked over and shook hands with Barbara. Winston and Prudence sniffed each other.

"Gosh, I feel a little let down," Nans said.

"Me too. I think Millie deserves a break since she was nice enough to return the K-Cups," Helen said.

"Millie was a good guy, and I like a happy ending where the good guy gets rewarded." Ida picked another cookie off the plate and bit into it. "It's kind of disappointing. I wonder if she'll have to move out of town now."

"She's not going to have to move." Mario had appeared at Ruth's side.

"Why not?" Nans asked.

"The Circo Acrobato family has decided to institute a pension plan, and Millie is one of the beneficiaries. She should be able to live quite comfortably at her little place in the retirement village for the rest of her life." Mario looked rather pleased about this.

Ida frowned. "A pension plan? You mean like you get when you retire from a big company?"

Mario nodded. "The Circo Acrobato is a company of sorts, and we are family, and—as my nephew William pointed out—family takes care of family."

"That's very nice of you, Mario." Ruth beamed up at him, and he slipped his arm around her shoulders.

"Aww, see, a happy ending. That feels much nicer. I think this calls for a piece of cake." Ida moved over to the other end of the table, where the slices of cake were set out, just as Millie and Winston joined them.

Lexy bent down to pet the dog. "You did good, Winston. You're a champ."

"Second place is pretty good!" Millie pointed to the red ribbon she'd clipped onto her lapel, and Lexy noticed a beautiful antique garnet brooch next to it.

"Did you get some of your jewelry back?" Lexy pointed to the brooch.

Millie looked down at it and smiled. "Yes! I had enough money to buy my stuff back, and Jeffrey was happy to sell them back for what he'd paid. He didn't charge extra or anything. I'm just glad it hadn't been sold."

"He's a very nice man." Ruth elbowed Ida in the ribs.

Millie turned to Helen. "Sorry about that K-Cup incident. I didn't mean any harm, really. It's so hard to go without coffee, and I figured there were so many in stock that no one would miss the few I borrowed. I always intended to replace them."

"No worries," Helen said.

"Well, looks like all the mysteries have been solved to our satisfaction," Ruth said.

Nans sighed. "It does look that way, but there's one problem. Now that all the mysteries are solved, how in the world are we going to entertain ourselves?"

****

Sign up for my VIP reader list and get my books at the lowest discount price:
https://lexybakerseries.gr8.com

Join my Facebook readers group and get special content and the inside scoop on my books:
https://www.facebook.com/groups/ldobbsreaders

If you want to receive a text message on your cell phone for new releases, text COZYMYSTERY to 88202 (sorry, this only works for US cell phones!)

American Buttercream Frosting

AMERICAN BUTTERCREAM FROSTING

American buttercream frosting is the sweet confection that most of us in the States grew up with. It's great for piping and delicious on any cake. The base vanilla flavor can be tweaked easily to add a different color or flavoring.

Ingredients:

2 sticks unsalted butter, room temperature

Pinch of salt

4 cups confectioners' sugar

2 teaspoons vanilla extract (or other flavoring—try almond or maple!)

1 to 2 tablespoons cream

. . .

Directions:

Put the butter in a large bowl and whisk until creamy.

Reduce mixer speed to low and add pinch of salt, then add sugar, one cup at a time, until well mixed.

Increase speed and add vanilla (or other flavoring) and 1 tbsp cream.

Whip for 2 minutes, continuing to add cream as needed.

Swiss Meringue Buttercream Frosting

S WISS M ERINGUE B UTTERCREAM Frosting

Swiss meringue buttercream is silky smooth and perfect for filling or frosting layers. It's a bit more work than other frostings since it involves cooking egg whites. I've heard you can skip the cooking step by using pasteurized egg whites, but Lexy would never skip a step.

Ingredients:

6 egg whites
    2 cups granulated sugar
    3 sticks unsalted butter, cut into tablespoons
    1 1/2 teaspoons vanilla extract
    Pinch salt

. . .

Directions:

Separate the eggs.

Whisk the sugar into the egg whites in a metal or heatproof bowl.

Place the bowl over a pot of simmering water. Do not let the bottom of the bowl touch the water. Whisk for about 4 minutes until the sugar is dissolved and the mixture has thinned. (If using a thermometer, it should be 160°F (71°C).)

Remove from heat and mix on medium high (while still warm) until stiff, glossy peaks form. This will take about 10 or 15 minutes.

Wait for bowl to cool and add butter, one tablespoon at a time.

Once the butter is fully mixed in, beat in the vanilla and salt.

FRENCH BUTTERCREAM FROSTING

French buttercream frosting is light and not overly sweet. It's the most difficult to make and uses egg yolks, which make it rich and custardy.

Ingredients:

6 egg yolks

2 whole eggs

1 1/2 cups granulated sugar

1/3 cup water

Pinch salt

3 sticks unsalted butter, cut into tablespoons

1 teaspoon vanilla extract

. . .

Directions:

Whisk whole eggs and yolks on medium-high speed for 5 minutes until mixture is thick and pale yellow.

Heat sugar and water in a medium pan over medium heat. Attach a candy thermometer and bring to 240°F without stirring (soft ball stage).

Whip eggs again on medium high and drizzle the hot sugar mixture into the eggs. Mix for 10 to 15 minutes until bowl is cool and mixture is thick but not yet forming stiff peaks.

Beat in the salt, then add the butter, 1 tablespoon at a time, while beating on medium high. Add vanilla extract once butter is incorporated.

Lexy Baker

Cozy Mystery Series

* * *

Killer Cupcakes

Dying For Danish

Murder, Money and Marzipan

3 Bodies and a Biscotti

Brownies, Bodies & Bad Guys

Bake, Battle & Roll

Wedded Blintz

Scones, Skulls & Scams

Ice Cream Murder

Mummified Meringues

Brutal Brulee (Novella)

No Scone Unturned

Cream Puff Killer

Never Say Pie

Aint Seen Muffin Yet

Assault and Buttercream

Kate Diamond Mystery Adventures

***

Hidden Agemda (Book 1)

Ancient Hiss Story (Book 2)

Heist Society (Book 3)

Oyster Cove Guesthouse

Cat Cozy Mystery Series

***

A Twist in the Tail

A Whisker in the Dark

A Purrfect Alibi

Silver Hollow

Paranormal Cozy Mystery Series

***

A Spell of Trouble (Book 1)

Spell Disaster (Book 2)

Nothing to Croak About (Book 3)

Cry Wolf (Book 4)

Shear Magic (Book 5)

Mooseamuck Island

Cozy Mystery Series

* * *

A Zen For Murder

A Crabby Killer

A Treacherous Treasure

Blackmoore Sisters

Cozy Mystery Series

* * *

Dead Wrong

Dead & Buried

Dead Tide

Buried Secrets

Deadly Intentions

A Grave Mistake

Spell Found

Fatal Fortune

Hidden Secrets

Hazel Martin Historical Mystery Series

***

Murder at Lowry House (book 1)

Murder by Misunderstanding (book 2)

Lady Katherine Regency Mysteries

***

An Invitation to Murder (Book 1)

The Baffling Burglaries of Bath (Book 2)

Sam Mason Mysteries

(As L. A. Dobbs)

***

Telling Lies (Book 1)

Keeping Secrets (Book 2)

Exposing Truths (Book 3)

Betraying Trust (Book 4)

Contemporary Romance

***

Reluctant Romance

Sweet Romance (Written As Annie Dobbs)

Firefly Inn Series

***

Another Chance (Book 1)

Another Wish (Book 2)

Hometown Hearts Series

***

No Getting Over You (Book 1)

A Change of Heart (Book 2)

Romantic Comedy

***

Corporate Chaos Series

In Over Her Head (book 1)

Can't Stand the Heat (book 2)

What Goes Around Comes Around (book 3)

Careful What You Wish For (4)

***

Sweetrock Sweet and Spicy Cowboy Romance

Some Like It Hot

Too Close For Comfort

———

Regency Romance

* * *

Scandals and Spies Series:

Kissing The Enemy

Deceiving the Duke

Tempting the Rival

Charming the Spy

Pursuing the Traitor

Captivating the Captain

The Unexpected Series:

An Unexpected Proposal

An Unexpected Passion

Dobbs Fancytales:

Dobbs Fancytales Boxed Set Collection

———

Western Historical Romance

***

Goldwater Creek Mail Order Brides:

Faith